MW01256577

STEEL EMPIRE

BRI BLACKWOOD

BRETAGEY PRESS

Copyright © 2021 by Bri Blackwood

This is a work of fiction. Names, characters, places, and incidents either are
the product of the author's imagination or are used fictitiously. Any
resemblance to actual persons, living or dead, events, or locales is entirely
coincidental. For more information, contact Bri Blackwood.

No part of this book may be reproduced in any form or by any electronic or
mechanical means, including information storage and retrieval systems,
without written permission from the author, except for the use of brief
quotations in a book review.

The subject matter is not appropriate for minors. Please note this novel
contains sexual situations, violence, sensitive and offensive language, and
dark themes. It also has situations that are dubious and could be triggering.

First Digital Edition: May 2021

Cover Designed by Amanda Walker PA and Design

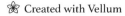 Created with Vellum

NOTE FROM THE AUTHOR

Hello!

Thank you for taking the time to read this book. Steel Empire is a dark billionaire romance. It is not recommended for minors and contains adult situations that are dubious and could be triggering. It isn't a standalone and the book ends with a happily ever after. Make sure you read Savage Empire and Scarred Empire before reading this book. The next book in the series is Shadow Empire.

Chapter Twenty-One might be triggering to some who have a sensitivity to guns. If you do, please skip or skim the chapter.

BLURB

Our bond is steel.

We began to rebuild what we had,
    Because I'm determined to make things right.
    Someone is out to ruin me,
    And they're using Anais to do it.
    Danger threatened to take her from me forever.
    But what they don't know,
    Is when someone threatens what is mine,
    There will be hell to pay.

PLAYLIST

Stronger (What Doesn't Kill You) - Kelly Clarkson
Confident - Demi Lovato
you should see me in a crown - Billie Eilish
Battle Symphony - Linkin Park
How to Save a Life - The Fray
Locked out of Heaven - Bruno Mars
It Ends Tonight - The All-American Rejects
Good Girls Go Bad - Cobra Starship, Leighton Meester
Death of a Bachelor - Panic! At The Disco
End Game - Taylor Swift, Ed Sheeran, Future
Safe and Sound - Capital Cities
Clovers. - JoJo

The playlist can be found on Spotify.

1

DAMIEN

The demons that haunted my nightmares were supposed to remain there.

Yet, they had materialized into the real world and stole what was mine. There wasn't much I feared, but my life had been turned upside down twice in recent weeks.

When Kingston alerted me that there was an incident involving Anais and her father and that his team was rushing in, my heart felt as if it were being strangled. It took precious moments for me to reach Rob and head down to the car because there was no way I would stay at my office waiting for word on what happened to Anais. Every second that passed without word made my mind race, wondering if the moment she walked out of my parents' home would be the last time I saw her. After I was told that although James had been shot, Anais was fine and they were transporting her to a safe house, I felt as if I could breathe again.

Once it was confirmed that Kingston had Anais and she was safe, I knew that everything was going to be fine. I trusted

Kingston with my life, and I knew that he would do every-thing in his power to make sure that Anais was okay.

The slight tremble of my hand as I pulled at my tie told me my feelings about this were completely different. The item of clothing now felt as if it were restricting my breathing, a change from just before I entered my home. The headache that was starting to form would not deter me from what had now become my only purpose: saving her.

Someone kidnapped her and I would drag whoever did this through the bowels of hell to get her back. This was a war and there wasn't a chance that I would lose.

I pulled my phone out again and clicked a single button to redial the number that I practically had memorized due to how many times I had seen it in the last hour, but I got the same thing every time: Anais's voicemail. I called both Kingston's and Carter's phones and got the same result. *Where the fuck is everyone?*

I cussed at myself for not working faster. The extra secu-rity measures that were supposed to be in place weren't due to be installed until Monday. *I'm failing her.*

My phone ringing brought me out of the spiraling that my mind was determined to take. "Damien."

"Mr. Cross?"

"Yes?"

"I just emailed you all of the security footage that we had from today. Is there anything else I can get for you?"

At least someone is responding. "That will be all for now. Thank you."

As I hung up and placed my phone down on the counter in front of me it rang, making me jump slightly. My brief hope that it was Anais was dashed when I looked at the caller ID.

"Where are you?" I couldn't stop the agitation in my voice because I knew time waited for no one.

"I'm almost at your place. I swung by on the way from New Jersey and picked up Broderick and Gage. We should be there in fifteen."

My fury increased with every word Kingston said. "Good. And be prepared to explain why you were in New Jersey and not here protecting Anais." I hung up the phone, not giving him a chance to respond. I could have been more understanding, but I didn't give a fuck. I wanted answers and I wanted them now.

Anais. Everything in me circled around thoughts of her. How I made a vow to fix things with her and show her the life we could lead together. Yet, someone was determined to stop that from happening.

If the unthinkable happened at the end of all of this, the biggest regret I would always carry with me was not having told Anais I loved her. My stomach almost revolted at the thought. A light cough left my mouth as I tried to contain my emotions, the silence of the suite almost too much to bear.

My eyes drifted back to the piece of paper sitting on my kitchen counter. This short letter was signed by a woman who I thought was dead. It did cross my mind that it could be someone playing a practical joke. After all, the letter was typed, not handwritten, so it would be hard to tell if this came from Charlotte herself.

But the sunflower that came with it was a trigger. Hell, the sunflowers from the day before tore through my mind as if a bomb had detonated. I felt as if I had seen a ghost when they were delivered to Anais. That should have been a sign that this wasn't anything to be taken for granted, but our intel had taken too long to make any connections before disaster hit. Where the hell was Carter?

The whiskey in my cabinet was tempting, begging me to give in to its lure, but I refused. Nothing would distract me from getting Anais back where she belonged: here with me.

Hindsight slapped me in the face and had its way of making one feel foolish. I had spent most of my time thinking that all of this was the result of a bad transaction that James Monroe had made. But I was wrong. Guilt rushed through my mind because I now knew that the person who had taken Anais had done it to hurt me.

As I grabbed my laptop to check the security footage, I thought of all the ways that this could have been prevented. My past was finally catching up with me and I needed to know who this was and what their motives were.

Images from the night of the fire flashed through my mind as I tried to focus on the task at hand. There was no way that Charlotte could have survived the fire. Who would try to play this fucked-up game? Whoever it was, they weren't going to get away with it.

A shot of adrenaline pulsed through my veins as my eyes scoured the video in front of me, trying to see if I could spot anything that might provide a clue for us to go on. But before I pressed play, I had a feeling I would find nothing. If the kidnapper was smart, they would have done the same thing that Anais had when she slipped out. The garage provided a perfect opportunity to leave unnoticed.

Unless my eyes were lying to me, my assumptions were correct. I didn't see anything on the video that would give even a sliver of a hint as to what happened to Anais. Unless someone had eyes on the penthouse, very few people knew about the blind spot in the garage, which forced me to consider Carter as the prime suspect. His lack of response meant that either he was incapacitated in some way, or he was the one who had kidnapped Anais.

Could this be Will's response to my killing Jon? That wasn't out of the realm of possibility but for him to have carried this out so quickly would have meant that he already had someone following me for a while. Plus, I knew this wasn't really his style. While I was prepared to face whatever he did after I killed one of his men, I suspected that he would let it be known that he had done it instead of playing mind games like this. Why would he pretend that his dead sister was alive?

That was the first time in a long time that I thought about Will and Charlotte as siblings. I ran a hand through my hair, walked over to the letter, and read it once more. I lived my life doing what I wanted whenever I wanted, no matter the cost. *What did Charlotte warn me about all those years ago that I didn't adhere to?*

I looked at my phone, but saw nothing on the screen indicating any changes to the situation I found myself in. I walked into my office and opened a drawer I knew all too well. Inside was a medium-sized black box that I pulled out and placed on my work surface. Once I put my thumb on the track pad and heard the lock disengage, I lifted the top of the case open and took out my pistol. I double-checked that the safety was on before I grabbed my holster and put it on my waistband. I hoped I wouldn't have to use it, but I was prepared to. Nothing was stopping me from getting Anais back in my arms.

Adrenaline raced through me as I walked back into the living area. I glanced at the note on the counter, but my head swerved when I heard a knock at my door. I walked over and flipped the lock before I swung open the door. I wasn't shocked to find Broderick, Gage, and Kingston on the other side. "We need to figure this out. If you have any intel, speak now," I said, not giving anyone else a moment to respond. "I'm determined to get Anais home as soon as possible."

I didn't expect my brothers to have any answers since they hadn't been at my side or with Anais these past few days the way Kingston had. The three men walked into the penthouse and my brothers sat down on the couch. Images of how Anais loved to curl up on the cushion closest to the window flashed through my mind. It was one of the many places in here that I knew I would always find Anais's presence, whether it was because of the scent of her shampoo or her leaving a book behind. Kingston walked over to the kitchen counter, dropped the bag that he had brought with him, and picked up the letter. I waited a beat before I cleared my throat and he looked up.

"We don't have time to waste," I said to Kingston. "What forced you to leave Anais here? And where the hell is Carter?" My anger was rising to the surface, but I did my best to restrain it. Keeping a cool head right now would be best for everyone.

Kingston flinched slightly before squaring his shoulders, ready for battle. Deep down, I knew there had to be a good reason why he hadn't been with Anais, but I also knew I wasn't going to like the answer. Especially since the end resulted in her being who knows where. A part of me was afraid, but I wouldn't admit to it.

"Our deal when we first talked about me protecting Anais was that if I were called away for anything, someone else on her detail would take over until I came back. That was the case today."

I leaned back on the kitchen counter and folded my arms. Where was this going?

"I was called away to New Jersey this morning, due to an emergency at one of the satellite offices. We thought it might have been a hack and I needed to be on site to make sure that the protocols that we had in place were being followed and none of our data leaked. So, I asked for Carter to be the one to come up and check on Anais and the suite. We didn't think this was related to you at all and my trip was supposed to be relatively quick. The plan was that I would be around to do the next shift before you got home, but I was further delayed by some other issues that came up as a result of the mayhem this 'hack' caused. This happened on my watch and I take full responsibility. You know I'll be standing right by your side to get her back."

I looked around the room and watched as the twins nodded after Kingston finished speaking. The deep breath that left my lungs was a result of me choking up and trying to quell my rage. The urge to punch my fist through the wall was there, but it wouldn't get us anywhere, and I knew that my family would stop at nothing to rectify this situation. "Where is Carter now? He was the last person to see Anais." I paused and my eyes were on Kingston. "What do you mean a hack?"

Kingston nodded and ran a hand through his dark blond

hair. "Turns out the hackers didn't actually steal any information, nor did they really try to. It was just enough to get everyone's attention and to keep us spinning our wheels for a few hours. That is also getting sorted back at the office. We are trying to figure out how they were able to pull that off, but that's for me to worry about since we have more pressing matters here. I ran a scan to see if I could track both Carter's work cell phone and his personal one, and they both seemed to be turned off, but my team will continue to ping both of those phones along with Anais's to see if either of them are turned back on. We're also doing another deep dive into Carter's background. I'm sorry, man."

"You followed the plans we had in place in case an emergency came up. We didn't know that someone on the team would go rogue. I think I was the last person to hear from her, at least out of everyone in this room."

I checked my phone for messages from her and I noticed Gage moving out of the corner of my eye. When I looked up, I saw that he had grabbed Anais's laptop and was walking over to Kingston. "This might provide some answers about what she was doing if she was working just before Carter showed up."

Why didn't I think of that? "That makes sense. That fucker...when I get my hands on him, he's dead." I meant that with every fiber of my being.

Gage handed the laptop to Kingston, who brought it to the kitchen counter. His hands flew across the keyboard. "Can you hand me that bag on the floor? It has my laptop in it." Gage bent down and handed him the bag. I looked over Kingston's shoulder and found him already on her computer.

"How did you know the password?"

"She had muted a video that was playing and since it was the top window open, her laptop never went to sleep. Saved us a bit of time from having to try to figure out her password."

Broderick walked over to see what Kingston was doing and the three of us looked on as our cousin worked some magic on Anais's laptop, hoping for a lead.

"Is that a group chat?" Broderick asked, pointing to a page near the corner of the screen.

Kingston tilted his head. "It looks like she was in a chat with a few of her coworkers. The only names I recognize are Vicki and Jake. The last message she sent was at 11:33 a.m. and she had a meeting on her calendar that ended just before that. Carter was supposed to check on her around noon, so this leads me to believe she was taken between 11:35 and noon."

His words further fed my anger, yet a sense of dread crept into my mind. She had been gone for hours and none of us had been the wiser. I should have checked in on her, but I had been so focused on closing the deal to buy her office building that I hadn't thought to text her after our midmorning messages. "Yeah, she works tirelessly so I can't imagine her not responding to any messages if everything had been okay." I looked over and checked the clock on the wall. "Carter and whomever else he is working with or for currently have about a six-and-a-half-hour head start on us."

Broderick raised an eyebrow at me. "Are you sure that he's working with someone else?"

I slightly nod. "Based on the attention that was given to making it seem as if Charlotte was alive, I would say so. How would he know about her? Either he did his research, or someone informed him about what happened all those years ago."

Gage and Broderick shared a look. Only they knew what the other was thinking. Some things never changed.

I sighed and looked at Kingston. "Did you find anything else?"

"I'm working on it," Kingston replied. Then he made a noise that sounded like he was hesitant to share it. He switched to his laptop for a moment before turning back to Anais's.

"What's wrong?"

"I might have some information that could help us track her down."

"Any information is good since we don't have much to go on at this point. I want all the information that your team has on Anais, myself, Carter, and anything anyone can tell us about Carter as soon as possible. Even if someone on your team thinks that something is pointless, I want it. I want to have everything in place because questions are going to start coming up and I will need to talk to her parents." I muttered a cuss word. "Once I tell them, they are probably going to want to go to the police, which may or may not be helpful depending on who orchestrated this. In my opinion, whoever did this was sending a message to me specifically and the less we tell the authorities, the better."

Someone took the woman I couldn't get enough of because of me, and it was due to something Charlotte told me during the brief time that we had dated. The letter from "Charlotte" proved that and I didn't have time to sit here and think about what she told me back in high school. What I did know was that no one ever took or disrespected what was mine and survived. I could wait on the police to investigate, but I liked taking matters into my own hands.

Ding.

The sudden noise came from Kingston's laptop and he shifted his body to look at the screen.

"Here are all of Charlotte's known living associates. I also pulled a list of people we looked into when we were looking at Carter." We rushed over to his computer and read it from over his shoulder.

"Okay," I said, scanning Charlotte's file before my eyes darted to Carter's. I wasn't shocked to see a couple of the names on Charlotte's list, because I had met several of them during the time that we dated. Carter's was a different matter. "Wait a minute. Jacob Doherty? She has a co-worker named Jake..."

I turned so that I could look at Anais's computer again. "I'm sure there was a Jacob or a Jake that popped up in the group chat conversation that Anais was having before she was taken?"

Kingston's, Broderick's, and Gage's gazes moved to Carter's file. Kingston's finger was hovering over the trackpad before he clicked on Jacob's name.

There it was.

He worked at Monroe Media Agency and to make matters worse he was a subordinate of Anais's. That more than likely meant over the time they had worked together, a sense of trust and mutual respect developed between the two. Jake temporarily lived with Carter when he first moved to the city years ago. I was willing to bet this penthouse that because of their connection and Jake's position at Monroe Media, Carter had recruited him to help him get closer to Anais in the workplace. *Fuck.*

"Anais told me that Jake threw Edward, a representative of one of Monroe Media Agency's clients, out of the office. Saying that while he preferred to talk to Anais, he had become increasingly more erratic since her father's shooting. As I mentioned before, I checked into it, but found nothing that would make me think that he had anything to do with this. What if all of that was bullshit and he threw the client's name out there to throw her, and therefore us, off the scent?"

"Would also explain the delivery of the gun to her office." I grabbed the letter from "Charlotte" and said, "Looks like we need to pay Jake a visit."

2

DAMIEN

"Anything there?" I said, checking to see if Kingston was able to spot anyone in the apartment that we were looking into. I was ready to storm in there like I owned the place. Hell, after this was all said and done, I might own it.

"No. Based on the evidence we have, Jake lives alone."

I knew double-checking things before we went in there made sense even if my patience was wearing thin. The longer we sat here staring at this fucker's window, the longer it took for us to get to Anais.

"All right let's go," I said, hitting the button to unlock the car door.

Kingston locked it again with a quick click. This might be the one time where having automated locks was detrimental.

"Wait." Kingston's voice stopped me. "Let's wait one more minute to make sure before we go in there like *Rambo*."

I knew what he was saying made sense. He was very particular about how he did things in his work and personal life, so I knew he wanted to be thorough. I also knew that he took Carter being the culprit extremely seriously because he was one of his men. "This better be the quickest minute of your life."

Kingston shook off my comment with a shrug. "Carter's not going to have a life worth living, but you need to let me do my job." Kingston glanced at me before turning his attention back to the window.

I looked through the rear-view mirror and found the twins staring intently out the window, not wanting to get in the middle of whatever Kingston and I were doing. I also didn't want to mention to anyone in the car that I had no intention of letting Carter live to see another day after I got my hands on him, but we'd deal with that when the time came. I swear if a hair on her head was missing, I'd—

"Damien." My thoughts stopped when I turned to Kingston again. "Let's go."

I unlocked the passenger side door and left the first barrier that was blocking me from releasing my rage onto Jake's face. It took everything for me to not sprint across the street up to Apartment 3B and snap his neck. Based on what I saw on the outside, it wouldn't be that hard. The building needed to be completely renovated or it needed to be torn down and rebuilt. It wasn't hard to see that the worn-down structure was dingy even at night. The light hanging just above the door didn't have a light bulb in it and the light flickering just beyond the front door was in desperate need of repair. The fact that any owner would allow this building to get into such a state was despicable.

It didn't take long for us to make it up to his apartment. The janky lock on the front door of the apartment building was easy to open and us breaking and entering meant nothing to me.

I wondered if our heavy footsteps would have been a warning to him as we marched up the stairs, but it turned out that someone else in the building was either having a party or just playing very loud music. That would make things considerably easier because I knew this might get loud.

We stood outside for a moment and a quick head nod with Kingston, Broderick, and Gage confirmed that we were all ready. My fist pounded on the door and it creaked under the weight of my hand. I wondered how much effort it would take to rip it off its hinges. Broderick placed a hand on my shoulder when my fists pounded on the door too many times. I waited several seconds to see if we could hear anything, but all we heard was the loud music coming from the floor below. I waited for a brief pause in the music before lifting my fist and pounding again.

"Jake. We know you're in there. And if you don't want this door to be taken off the hinges, open. Up." My bellowing echoed in the hallway yet there was still no response.

"All right. The only way he hasn't heard us is if he's taking a shit," I said.

"We saw someone's shadow move back and forth across the window before we came up here. Someone's home," Gage said.

Broderick looked at the door, examining its sturdiness. "I think we could take this down." Before any of us could move the door swung open and it took me a millisecond to recover. Jake's eyes widened as he saw that there were four pissed-off men standing outside of his apartment and when his gaze landed on me, his eyes grew even larger. He backed up with his hands up.

"Listen, I didn't do anything. I have no idea why you're here. I've been just minding my business, dude."

The tremble in his voice annoyed me yet was satisfying. We made our way into his apartment and Kingston closed the door behind us. One glance around proved that the apartment was just as shitty on the inside as it was on the outside. Jake didn't help matters given how messy he kept his space. The fact that anyone could get away with this was mind blowing. When all of this was over, I made a note to myself to ask Melissa to report the state of this apartment to the city. Although Jake was on my shit list, that didn't mean the rest of the tenants deserved to suffer.

My dry chuckle made him jump. *Good.* "Why do I get the suspicion that you aren't just minding your business?" I said, mimicking the quivering that I heard in his voice. My eyes moved around the room, trying to see if I could spot Anais anywhere. "Stay here."

I searched from room to room but came up empty. Kingston, Broderick, and Gage followed suit when I returned. They tore through his apartment in a New York minute because that was all we had. When we came up empty-handed, I walked back over to Jake and levied a heavy glare at him. I folded my arms across my chest and stared at him.

"Where is Anais?"

"Who?"

I grabbed him by his shirt, lifted him up, and threw him against the wall. I could hear several stitches on his T-shirt ripping as I did. "Where is Anais Monroe? Don't act stupid with me," I said, making sure to enunciate each word perfectly, so there was no risk of misinterpreting.

He took a hard gulp and said, "I don't know who you're talking about."

"If you value your life, you won't want to fuck around with me right now. Where. Is. She?" I maneuvered so that my left arm was holding him up against the wall. I kept pressure on his neck and my body slightly shook because of the anger that was about to boil over. I could feel my sanity slipping through my fingers and it was only a matter of time before I was about to break. "Tell the truth."

His eyes moved down to my right fist, which was clenching. It should have served as a warning, but he didn't take heed to it. "I told you the truth. I don't know who Anais is."

That did it. The feeling of my right fist crushing his nose brought power and some pain but just hearing the crunch was satisfying. Gage tossed a paper towel at him, granting him more grace than I could muster in my pinky finger. I wanted to make his nose bleed even more. I held back and let him drop to the floor like a sack of potatoes.

"Ouch—Yes!" He tried his best to contain the blood and the nasally tinge to his voice that was both grating and satisfying. "I know Anais. She's my boss."

"Where is she?"

"What do you, uh, mean where is she? Last time I saw her was when there was a big deal over a package being delivered to the office and she was there. The l-last time I ran into her was when she was talking to Vicki after a meeting." His stammering was getting on my nerves. "I mentioned to her something about one of our clients who no matter how hard we tried always wanted to talk to her instead of someone else."

"And that's when you tried to throw this client under the bus and told Anais that his actions were escalating."

Jake didn't deny anything this time.

"Now if I have to repeat myself again and ask about Anais..."

"What do you know about Charlotte DePalma?" Broderick's question cut through the tension that was building in the room like a heated blade.

That question hit a nerve. Jake let out a curse, but it was mostly muffled by the blood spewing from his nose. "I've only briefly heard about her. Haven't seen or talked to her. Stop touching that!"

Gage stopped looking through the papers on Jake's desk. He sent a smirk over to Jake before he went back to searching through papers. That's when the light bulb went on in Jake's head. "Listen, I had nothing to do with any of this. M-my job was to spend the last few months keeping tabs on Anais and report anything I found to Carter. He was doing something similar, I assume, for whoever hired him. Carter was my contact, but I heard him mention something about reporting to his boss. Oh, I also was given a box and told to deliver it to Anais at the office. Never saw the guy who gave it to me before in my life."

And there is the confirmation we need. "So, your job was to stalk her and you're the reason why that gun popped up at Monroe Media Agency," I said before I shared a look with Gage.

His eyes darted toward Gage again before returning to me. "I wouldn't—" The words died on his lips. "Can I have a towel, please?"

Broderick came out of the bathroom, towel in hand. He

stared at Jake, almost daring him to do something before tossing a towel at him. The twins shared a look between each other.

Jake drew the towel up to his nose. "I think I need to go to the hospital."

"Don't care. How did you stalk Anais?"

"I might have followed her a few times and took pictures outside of her apartment window."

I saw red. "You fucking asshole!" I pulled my fist back, ready to land another hit, and he flinched back in response before attempting to cower.

"Damien, he's not worth it," Broderick said, saving Jake from another punch to his already busted face.

"Listen, I'm also the one that brought the box into Monroe Media Agency, but I didn't know what was in it. I swear that's all I did. Hey, I reported whatever I found to Carter by text message. I'll give you the number he gave me, and I'll also write down the address where I took photos of Anais. Carter gave me the key to an apartment, and it made things easier." He took a deep breath and visibly relaxed. "I'll give you everything and I swear I was never told about her disappearing. I only did this for some extra cash."

So, Jake was kept on a need-to-know basis. Smart, just in case he leaked any information. I took a step back, giving him an opportunity to get the things that he offered. He had nowhere to go but out the window, which would be a pretty steep drop. That was only if he made it past all four of us.

Jake walked over to a desk and flipped open a notebook. "It's around here somewhere," he muttered, as he moved on from the notebook and dug into one of his desk drawers.

"If you're trying to do something funny and pull out a

weapon, you'll be dead before you can blink." And I meant it. The fear I saw in his eyes was unmistakable when he briefly looked at me before returning to searching. My gut told me that he wasn't going to attempt to escape this situation, but I prepared myself just in case.

"Ah, here it is," he said, pulling out a torn piece of paper that clearly had seen better days. He turned it over and scribbled something down on it before handing it to me. I saw the phone number and the address and handed it to Kingston. "I need to go see someone about my nose. Fuck."

I ignored him. "Kingston, is this number registered to Cross Sentinel?"

"I'm almost positive it's not, but I'll double-check. Maybe we can pick up a signal from it." Kingston looked at me before looking at Jake and said, "I'll make a phone call and meet you in the car." He walked out with the piece of paper in hand.

I turned my attention back to Jake, who was holding out a key that I placed in my pocket. "If you hear from Carter at any point, you call me. If you tell anyone else what transpired here tonight, you're going to end up in the Hudson. Got me?" He nodded his head. "Definitely have your nose looked at, but you're lucky that's all that happened. You should probably start searching for a new job too."

With that, Broderick, Gage, and I filed out of Jake's tiny apartment and soon found ourselves entering Kingston's SUV. As we closed the doors, Kingston was wrapping up a phone call.

"So, Carter must have had a burner phone because just as I thought, that number didn't belong to us."

"Kingston, any updates on a signal from all of Carter's phones or Anais's?"

"Still nothing. Looks like the burner phone is off as well." Kingston pulled out of the parking spot and drove down the street. "I already put the apartment address that Jake gave us into the GPS. It shouldn't take us too long to get there."

I looked at the map on Kingston's screen and recognized the streets. "Hidden Tavern is on that corner. I think this building is near Anais's old apartment."

3
ANAIS

I could feel something wet falling on my face. *Am I outside? Is it drizzling? I can only hope that this is water.* I wanted to know what it was, but it took too much energy to open my eyes. It felt as if my body was being weighed down by something, pulling me further and further into the depths of the unknown. Visions of water surrounded me from all angles as I tried to fight, but nothing I did was helping to propel me in the opposite direction.

I yanked hard and felt something move, but there was no change. I tried again in an effort to potentially free myself. Nothing. I couldn't tell if I had imagined that I had moved or if I had made the motion. That was when I felt something hit me on my forehead. Then again and again.

Liquid? But I'm already surrounded by it. How can I feel drops of liquid on my face when I'm in the middle of the ocean battling to survive?

Yet the drops continued. I shifted and wiggled my fingers. The slight fidgeting led me to feel a cool hardness under my fingertips. *Am I on land? I think I'm lying on something hard.*

Coldness crept in as the pressure to keep my eyes closed eased yet opening them wasn't an option. Or so my body was telling me. The smell of mildew and something else I couldn't place filtered through my nostrils. A hazy feeling took over me as I tried to awaken my mind and body.

My eyes flickered when another drop landed on my forehead. *Where am I?*

A dull throbbing in my head took hold, yet, for some reason, I still couldn't open my eyes. I pulled all of my focus and energy away from identifying my surroundings by touch, smell, and hearing toward opening my eyes. A sudden noise that wasn't too far from me made me jump and adrenaline forced an eye open. However, I couldn't keep it open because the pain was intensifying and what felt like a jackhammer had made my head its home. *Am I alone?*

How I wished I weren't alone and instead back in Damien's arms. I held back a sob as a picture of Damien flashed through my mind. Would I ever see him again? Our relationship was reaching new heights and I could feel our partnership getting stronger. The vulnerability he displayed after he killed Jon, and the day the sunflowers were delivered, were just small snippets of the trust that had developed between us. Now, all of that was up in the air. The rush of emotion that I felt when I admitted to myself that I loved him hit me like a boulder and I fought the urge to cry.

I wondered if I had imagined the noise that I heard just a couple of minutes before. I thought about speaking to see if someone was there and could help me but keeping silent won over as I didn't want to alert anyone that I was awake and trying to pull myself together. Anything that might give my adversary the upper hand. I suppressed a groan and finally, I was able to open one of my eyes into a tiny slit and keep it open.

I was in what looked to be a dark room. My wobbly sight tried to focus on something but couldn't. The blurriness increased due to the blistering pain that was radiating through my skull. Unfortunately, that wasn't the only pain I was feeling. My body ached as if I'd just lost a fight. *What happened to me?*

I tried to force myself to open up my other eye, but it still felt too heavy. It was time to try something else. I slightly wiggled my feet, both seemed to be just fine, but when I tried to move my hands more, I froze. It hurt to move them and they were being restrained behind my back.

I heard another noise come from a corner of the room that I had no chance in hell of seeing. If I thought the first noise might have been a fluke, this one proved that I wasn't alone. Fear jolted my mind and body into action, and instinct called for me to flail my limbs to see if I could get up, but I refrained. Instead, I channelled my energy to slowly opening my other eye, allowing me to see my environment better. Part of me wanted to scream out for help, but fright kept a choke-hold on my vocal cords. I still had to squint both of my eyes, but at least I was able to use both of them.

What came into focus was the fact that I was in a small dark room. My first thought was that it had to be a basement given the lack of light and windows from what I could see. There were shadows in the distance that I couldn't make out and who knew what lurked in them. It differed from the plain room that Damien's men dragged me to right after my father was shot. The mildew and moldy smells were becoming suffocating, and the muskiness of the room increased not only my desire to figure out where I was but also the fear that was driving my heart to race.

My eyes opened a smidge wider as some of the memories flowed back into my consciousness. I remember being in Damien's penthouse and Carter coming up to the suite to tell me that Damien requested that I travel to his office to attend something related to his birthday. After I pulled myself together, I left the penthouse, but didn't pay attention to Carter as I locked the door. Then everything went black.

I should have known something was up, because Damien hadn't mentioned his birthday before he left the house. I blindly trusted Carter, who was supposed to protect me, and I shouldn't have.

I know I had been hit with something pretty heavy due to the headache I was sporting, unless it was from impact else-where. I wondered if I had a concussion, but those thoughts were cut short when I heard another noise from somewhere behind me. I tried to roll onto my back, but it was difficult given the placement of my hands.

These fucking zip ties again. If I never saw another one again if I got out of here, it would be too soon. I struggled against my bonds, secretly hoping, and praying that I would miraculously be free, but nothing happened.

Carter. Yes, we started out on the wrong foot after he led the team that snatched me out of harm's way and treated me more harshly than needed. I never would have thought that he would kidnap me and throw me back into peril. When I shifted my position, I almost cried out in pain. This time not from the throbbing in my head, but from an ache in my abdomen. It felt like I had been kicked there.

My brain struggled to figure out what his connection was

to the raspy-voiced man, but I hadn't a clue. I closed my eyes once more as the pounding in my head took over. *I need to get out of here.*

After several deep breaths, I opened my eyes again, hoping and praying that there was something I missed. Something that might aid me in getting out of here. Nothing but pitch blackness greeted me in return.

That was until I heard a slight commotion again. My stomach was in my throat as one word fell from my lips.

"Hello?"

4

DAMIEN

Kingston was right. We arrived in no time to an apartment building that looked almost identical to Anais's. When we opened the door, I shook my head, taking it all in. There was so much shit in the apartment that I knew it would take us a while to get through it all. Kingston must have reached the same conclusion because his hand immediately went for his phone and soon, he was calling for some members of his team to come to the apartment to do a more thorough search than we could do in the limited time we had. Every precious second wasted meant that Anais's life was in more danger.

The apartment was more of a studio. Carter and whoever he was working with had made sure to leave a mess. I flicked the switch, and a dullish light lit the room. The room was almost bare, from its off-white walls to the wooden floors that had seen better days. There was an almost-deflated air mattress in the room along with some food wrappers. Someone had lived here at least part-time.

"You've got to be kidding me," I said to no one in particular as I looked around the room. "It's clear he didn't have any time to clean anything out, so there might be something here. Just who knows what because of all of the shit we'll have to dig through."

"This might be a dead end."

I almost growled at Broderick, but he was right. This was looking more and more like a dead end.

"I won't rest until we find her."

"I know."

"There are some scraps left around so maybe something is here to tell us where he took Anais," said Kingston, interrupting my conversation with Broderick.

I hoped he was right.

"I'm going to stand guard at the door right here and keep watch."

I nodded at Broderick and the rest of us started digging through the papers and other items that we found. It was clear that someone had left in a hurry. If this space was indeed Carter's, I hoped that him kidnapping Anais wasn't a well-thought-out plan and that he had made a few mistakes that we could find.

"Someone's coming."

"Can you see who they are?"

"No. It's too dark."

A crash at the door caused both Kingston and me to draw our weapons. Broderick took a few steps back to line up with us before the intruders came in. I wish I could say I was surprised to see Will and his men standing before me, but I wasn't. It was only a matter of time before he would appear, and he couldn't have had worse timing. I also wasn't surprised that the two men that followed him into the room had their weapons drawn as well.

"What are you doing here, Will?"

"I think you know why I'm here."

I took a step toward him, ready for battle. "Where is Anais?"

Will held up his hands, while his guys behind him strengthened the hold they had on their guns. "What do you mean where is Anais?"

"This is not the time to fuck around with me. Where is she?"

"I have no idea what you're talking about. I'm here about Jon. Someone told me they saw him go into a warehouse the other night and not come back out. Your cousin over there owns said warehouse so it doesn't take much to put together what happened. I've had eyes on you ever since."

"You knew he had it coming. You should be thanking me."

Will shrugged. "He might have, but he was still a member of the Vitale family and it's up to us to take out our own trash. You should have just come and talked to me."

I adjusted my stance, my finger firmly on the trigger. "I know the Vitale family also does their damnedest to protect their women. I was protecting mine. He had plenty of warning to stop his behavior and refused." I knew I didn't have to explain myself to Will, but I didn't want to kill him. This standoff was causing me to lose even more time. The longer we had to stand here and deal with this, the more danger Anais was in. "We can hash this out at another time."

"But I want to 'hash' this out right now."

"Will, I don't have the time to deal with this—"

"Is it because your fiancée is missing?"

My shoulders tensed as his words floated around the room, but I didn't respond.

"Looks like one of the big dogs has suddenly become extremely vulnerable. What a perfect time to use this to my advantage."

I glanced at Gage, who was standing to my left. I could see that he was itching to make a move but I didn't know if he was armed because Kingston and I were the only ones who drew our weapons. "Did you take Anais?"

Will scoffed. "You would have known if I had. I don't exactly shrink off and hide from my actions. But now you must answer for what you've done to Jon. Family above all else, right? Put the gun down."

"Don't do it, Damien." Broderick's voice seemed a million miles away as I stared down the three men in front of me. Would putting my gun down get us out of here faster? I was also risking my life and the lives of my family if I did what Will asked.

"Put the gun down." His words came out low, almost daring me to disobey.

"Don't listen to him!"

My thoughts were at war with one another as I struggled to rise above the madness that had been a result of my own doing. I was the one who brought Anais into this; I was the one who killed Jon. And Will did have the upper hand here. But there was one card I hadn't played yet, and I knew once I did, that it would flip everything.

"Anais received sunflowers yesterday."

Will's eyebrow rose. "And what does that have to do with anything? Did she have a secret admirer, ready to swoop in once you threw her to the wolves?"

I kept a cool head, although it was tempting to rise to the bait that Will had just thrown out there. "No. But when I arrived home this evening and found that Anais was missing, I did find a note that was left behind. The note was signed with Charlotte's name."

I could see when my words registered in his mind. "Damien, I didn't think you would stoop so fucking low to lie about—"

"I'm not lying. Pull the piece of paper out of my back pocket."

Will shared a look with his guardsmen before walking around and coming toward me. Kingston and I still had our guns trained on the men in front of us who were ready to answer any gunfire with a response of their own. I knew I was giving Will an opportunity to assault me, but it was a risk I was willing to take. Anything that might lead to this stalemate ending and giving us an opportunity to get out of here and deal with the people we needed to deal with.

Will snatched the piece of paper out of my back pocket before taking a large step back from me. I held back the sigh of relief that was on my lips because he hadn't thrown a cheap shot in order to get me to drop my gun.

"You're telling the truth, but this has to be a lie. We both know that Charlotte is dead."

Will walked back into my field of vision and I could see that some of the confidence that he walked in here with had diminished.

"I don't know what this means yet but somehow, Charlotte is connected to Anais's disappearance and—"

"SHUT UP!" Will's words were raw and emotional. Something that I hadn't seen since the day of Charlotte's funeral. It was easy to hear his labored breathing in the silence of the room.

When it seemed that he wouldn't be saying anything else, I spoke up. "I know I'm the last person you want to deal with right now and you want revenge because I killed one of your guys. But if there is a shot that we can save my fiancée and your sister, we need to do this."

Will's eyes hadn't left the piece of paper, but he didn't say anything after I made my proposal. I started to wonder if he had gone into shock.

"Boss? What do you want us to do?" The man standing over Will's left shoulder spoke, asking the question we all wanted to hear the answer to.

"If you can promise me that we can find out about what happened to Charlotte and how she's tied into this, I'll spare your life."

"Deal," I said. "Now have your men drop their weapons and we'll drop ours." I allowed the words to pass over my lips, not knowing if I was telling the truth or not.

I could feel the power dynamic in the room shift as Will considered my words. He looked at the men standing over his shoulder and gestured for them to lower their guns. It took a moment for each man to comply, but once they did, Kingston and I followed suit.

"What can we do to help?"

What Will said was like music to my ears. "We need help digging through all of this stuff. We are looking for something that might give us a hint as to where Anais might be. If Charlotte is alive and involved in any of this at all, my gut tells me we will find out once we find Anais."

Will nodded his head. "But don't forget what I said. If this is a wild goose chase, I'm shooting you myself."

"Do you think I would lie about something like this?"

Will took two steps toward me and we were only standing about a foot apart. "No. But I know that people get desperate when they are backed into a corner. And that's where you are."

With a nod of his head, he gestured for his men to follow him and as the men walked around me, I put my gun away. The studio apartment didn't hold much in the way of furniture. Aside from the air mattress there was an old desk in the corner, and I headed over to it. Everyone spread out and looked through all of the crap that Carter and any of his accomplices left behind.

"Kingston," I said without looking up from the task at hand. "When are your men supposed to get here?"

"Not for another twenty to thirty minutes or so."

I wanted to be out of here by the time they arrived, with our next location in hand. Having them in here with us would only cause even more confusion and there was no way all of us would be able to fit in this small space. It was already a struggle with the seven of us here.

I was scanning through the papers in my hand when Gage said, "I found something."

I never knew those three words would cause my heart to careen out of control, but I bolted over to him and everyone else followed me. I looked at the pieces of paper in his hands. They were receipts from a hardware store and a grocery store in Gray, New Jersey. "It might be a long shot, but it might be a lead. Looks like he might have been preparing for something."

Normally I wouldn't have automatically assumed that someone stopping in a store in a random town would mean that they were staying there. But since this was the only lead we had, and that grocery list looked particularly long, it was worth a shot.

"Are you coming along?" My gaze left the receipts and drifted toward Will.

"Yes."

5

ANAIS

"Hello?" I asked, repeating what I said because I didn't get an answer the first time. My voice was nothing more than a croak. I decided to switch tactics because I needed to find out what was making noise in that dark abyss. I heard some rifling in the distance and panic set in. Was there a creature down here with me? After all they wouldn't be able to respond in words to me...

"Hi," came a soft voice laced with a hint of scratchiness, but full of relief.

My heart raced as I tried to make sense of it all. Fogginess clouded my mind as I tried to piece together the information I had. Who was this person and how were they involved in all of this?

"Who are you?" I asked, not wanting to trust that they were a prisoner like me.

"My name is Jenna." Her voice sounded a little stronger, but hesitant. "I thought you were dead."

"I feel that way if that's any consolation."

I could hear more movement and a few seconds later a

figure appeared. A woman with lighter colored hair that reached a few inches past her shoulders leaned down in front of me. I pulled away from her, weary that she might hurt me instead of help.

"Where are we?" The scratchiness in my throat became more prevalent.

"No clue. I woke up down here just like you did except when I did it, there was no one here."

I muttered a curse and closed my eyes tight, before opening them back up. Unless this was a ploy to get me to trust her, I could confirm that she was in the same predicament as me. "Great."

"It's so nice to have someone else here, as bad as that sounds," she said. "Are you feeling okay?"

I groaned and tried to swallow. The dryness in my throat was making me uncomfortable, but it ranked low on the scale of things that were fucked up about this entire situation. "I understand what you mean. I might have a concussion. Blazing headache and my vision is still a bit blurry although it seems to be clearing up. Body is hurting too." I closed my eyes and tried to swallow once more.

"I heard him bring you in here and I did my best to check up on you when he left, but you wouldn't wake up. There wasn't much I could do with my hands tied behind my back."

I nodded and thankful that she had looked after me. Yet, I immediately regretted the decision to move my head. I hissed and winced.

"Be careful," she said before she plopped down on the ground next to me. It was clear she was in better shape to move around than I was.

I took a deep breath and let it out. "How long have you been here?"

"Um, I'm not sure. There are no windows in here. If I had to guess maybe a day or so."

"And I just got here according to your calculations."

"That's right."

"Then today is February 4th."

I heard her gasp and suck in a breath. "I've been here for two days."

I felt bad for her, but a small glimmer of hope popped into my mind. "Would anyone know that you're missing? Maybe someone called the cops and alerted them that you didn't go to work?"

I saw Jenna shift slightly. "Potentially, but more than likely it will be a while before they discover I'm missing."

Just as quickly, those hopes were dashed and I could only hope that by now, Damien was looking for me.

"It felt as if we traveled for hours before he brought me here. Of course, that could be wrong."

That was understandable, especially if she had been kidnapped in a similar manner to me. "Where do you live?"

"Small town in Pennsylvania. Not too far from Philly."

The east coast of the United States was pretty large, but I wanted to bet Carter and whoever else he might have been working with stashed us not too far from New York City or Philadelphia.

"I live in NYC so maybe we aren't too far from either place." I was trying to sit up and not having much luck.

"That's where I'm from originally. Oh, let me help," Jenna said as she let me use her body as leverage to help me sit up against the wall about six inches away.

I leaned my head back on the wall, the motions that we just made taking a lot of energy. After a few deep breaths, I felt comfortable opening my eyes again.

"Have you been able to find a way out? Would it be something we might be able to achieve together? If Carter is alone, we might be able to outmaneuver him."

"Is that his name? And no. It's useless to scream. When I first got here, I screamed off and on until my voice went hoarse. I tried it again just before he brought you down here, but to no avail."

Ah, that explained the soft yet roughness of her voice. Sitting up allowed me to get a better visual of the room. I wondered if we were underground. That would explain the lack of windows.

"I never got a chance to ask you if anyone would be looking for you?" Her voice grew with the same hopefulness that I had just moments before.

"Ah, yes. My parents will start questioning things within the next day or so since I call them a few times a week. My best friend will also start panicking because we text at least once a day. I also wouldn't be surprised if my fiancé was looking for me right now."

"Fiancé? At least you have someone to look to when we get out of here."

I didn't correct her because of course I couldn't tell her that my relationship with Damien was fake. I assumed at the very least he would want to rescue me because he didn't want to have to deal with being a prime suspect in a kidnapping investigation. I moved my fingers and that was when I realized that something was missing. "Shit."

"What's wrong?"

"My ring is missing. I either lost it when Carter kidnapped me, or he snatched it."

"I'm sorry."

I didn't tell her how much I despised it anyway, but not having it hurt me more than I was willing to admit. Since Damien was the one who gave it to me, I was willing to overlook the issues I had with it. That shook me.

"Anyway, the best bet is that my fiancé, Damien, will be the quickest to start searching for me."

Jenna joined me in lying back against the wall. "I knew a Damien once."

"Oh really?" My heart leaped into my throat. It couldn't be possible that we knew the same Damien, right? New York City was huge and I'm sure there were a ton of Damiens within the city limits. "What's his last name?"

I asked the question, not sure if I wanted to know the answer. I held my breath as I waited to hear her response.

"Cross. His name is Damien Cross."

6

DAMIEN

"Did you send any more of your men to protect Anais's parents?" I needed to reach out to my father to warn him as well.

Kingston nodded. "Sent that message when I was waiting for you all to leave Jake's apartment."

"And I just texted Dad about what was going on. They are on high alert as well," Broderick chimed in from the backseat.

Well at least I don't have to worry about that.

The ringing of my phone dragged my attention away and the caller ID showed that it was an unknown number with a New Jersey area code. I answered without even thinking, hoping that maybe it was Anais calling from another number. "Anais?"

"Is this Damien?" The female voice wasn't the one I was longing to hear.

"Yes. Who is this?" I didn't have time for games. At least I wasn't driving so this phone call wasn't hindering that.

"Hi, this is Ellie. I called to see if Anais was with you? She and I were supposed to talk this evening, but she never called me."

I sat up a little straighter, causing the seat belt to pull a little tighter. I paused before responding, trying to decide how I was going to word what I wanted to say. "Anais has been kidnapped." Any finesse that I wanted to have was long gone. Being blunt and getting straight to the point was the goal here. The quicker this conversation went, the better.

"What! Did you just say that she has been—" she said. Her voice became more high-pitched. "Wasn't it your job to protect her?"

Hearing someone else say the words that I had been using to beat myself up over the last few hours added to the sucker punch feeling that I was currently nursing. Everything she said was correct and once again thoughts of how I failed Anais flooded my brain.

"Listen, Damien, I shouldn't have said that. I assume that you wouldn't want anything—"

"You're damn right I wouldn't want anything to happen to her."

I heard what sounded like a sniffle before Ellie said, "Have you heard anything from Anais or the person who kidnapped her? Are there any r-ransom demands?"

"I haven't heard anything." Wouldn't now have been an ideal time to contact me about paying for her return? Maybe Carter and whomever he was working for weren't after money.

"So, we don't know if she's dead or alive." Her voice cracked at the end of her statement and it was easy to tell she was barely hanging on.

"Ellie, I'm going to get her back. I promise you this."

I heard some shuffling in the background before Ellie sighed on the other end of the line. "I know you will. Is there anything I can do to help?"

"As of right now, no. If Anais or someone else contacts you about her, call me immediately."

"O-okay." There was a brief pause on the other end of the line and then she continued, "Now I'm thankful that we didn't try to move me back to the city yet. Nick mentioned that it might be a few more days before it made sense for me to come back."

At the mention of her bodyguard's name, I looked up from my phone and turned to Kingston. Kingston nodded, confirming the information that Ellie shared.

Yet another thing I didn't know about Anais. Ellie's comment caused a new round of thoughts to pop into my head. Was it possible that Carter told someone else about his plans even if he was being vague about it?

"Who is Carter closest to, Kingston?"

"I assume he would be closer to a few of the guys on the team because he's been with us for a couple of years." He stopped and glanced out of the sideview mirror before he continued. "Maybe Nick. He has a knack for making friends with anyone. He's who we sent to watch Ellie."

"I'll ask Ellie to grab him." *This might be another break for us.* "Hey, Ellie?"

Her sniffling continued and I could tell she was attempting to calm herself down.

"Yeah?" Her voice was shaky, and I wondered if she would be able to hold it together for much longer.

"Is Nick near you now?"

"No. He's probably sitting in my parents' living room. I

had wondered why he decided to set up shop there a couple of hours ago, but it was because of all of this I assume," she mumbled as I heard a commotion in the background before Ellie said, "Here's Nick."

I put the phone on speaker and set it on the console.

"Okay, Nick. Kingston here. How close are you to Carter?"

"We talk on occasion. Have grabbed a couple of beers here and there when we were off the clock."

"Do you know anything about whether or not he had some sort of property close by? Within driving distance of New York City?"

"Yes. He mentioned having a place in Jersey. Some sort of cabin that he would go to when he had time off. He didn't refer to it as a vacation spot, just that he had a place where he could stay when he wanted to lay low. His goal is to retire and eventually move to an island and be away from the world."

Chances were that he didn't take Anais anywhere near an island, but I wanted to double-check one thing. "Did he ever mention where the cabin was?"

"Yes. Sorry, I'm blanking. It was something unusual. Not Orange, New Jersey..."

"Gray?"

"That's it."

"Address?"

"Not one that I know of. I also don't know if the property is in his name or not."

Kingston cleared his throat. "Nick, I'm sending backup your way just in case Carter or any associates of his try to cause any more shit."

"But I have a handle on everything—"

"Carter is considered armed and dangerous. He has

nothing to lose, and I don't want to lose anyone else. Copy that?"

"Yes."

I was thankful that we were already on our way to Gray. We didn't have an address, but at least we had an area. Maybe we might be able to talk to someone there and get directions.

Kingston placed more pressure on the gas, and we sped off to New Jersey, to a town that might be where Anais was being held captive.

7

ANAIS

Was it the concussion or did she really just say that she knew Damien Cross?

"How do you know him?"

"We dated a lifetime ago."

I raised an eyebrow. "How long is a lifetime?" My heart started racing as I waited for her answer.

"Our senior year of high school. We hadn't been dating for long, before something tragic happened, pulling us apart."

"You're Charlotte." I could barely see Jenna look down at her lap, her hair covering her face. I almost expected her to deny the claim, but she didn't. She sniffled and I continued, "Damien thinks you're dead."

"No one has called me Charlotte in well over a decade. And most people do think I'm gone." Another sniffle ended her sentence.

I wished I could have handed her a tissue, but I didn't have one and our hands were tied. The tone of her voice made the story sound believable, but I was still studious.

Here was a woman that was supposed to be dead for years due to a house fire, yet now I was supposed to believe that she was alive and well? I saw how much Damien was affected by her "death" and if she was telling the truth, I wished she would have told him that she was alive. At the very least, I knew I should be nice to her just in case she was involved in my kidnapping and maybe that would be enough to buy me time.

"Is it okay if I call you Charlotte?"

"Yes, I would like that."

"What happened? And how did you get here?"

"Since you know my real name, I assume Damien told you about what happened that night."

"Yes, he told me his version of events, but I want to hear from you."

"The whole thing was a setup."

"Wait, what?"

"I was forced to lure Damien there."

"Wait—What? Why would anyone want to kill Damien? He was only in high school."

"The long and short of it is that it all started with our parents. Martin Cross and my father, Harvey, were associates and did business together until my father died. One of my older brothers, Vincent, always blamed Martin for my father's death."

That's when it clicked. "And by killing Damien that was his way of getting back at him."

"Right. I just did as I was told. Well, sort of." She sighed again. "Vincent lost it when our father killed himself and with Will away at the time Vincent was my only guardian. Vincent was in and out of trouble as a teen and Dad always bailed him out. With him being the oldest child they were extremely close so when Dad passed I was shocked that he took it harder than both Will and me. Once the dust settled, he hatched this plan where I would start dating Damien and that later turned into the trip up to our vacation home in upstate New York. He threatened to kill me if I didn't do what he wanted."

Charlotte took a deep breath and continued, "A few days before heading upstate, I decided there was no way I could kill Damien and I came up with a plan. I gave Vincent the signal when I knew Damien was downstairs, hoping that it would give Damien an opportunity to get away because he was on the first floor instead of the second. I left my phone in the bedroom and tip-toed across the hall to the guest room with a small bag that I'd packed. I'd hoped and prayed that he would survive as I climbed through one of the windows in a guest bedroom and took off into the forest. I knew there was a chance that Vincent might kill me, so I kept going. I called the police from my burner phone and ditched it while I was travelling through the woods. I eventually made it to civilization and was able to disappear. I kept tabs on the news and everyone had assumed I died in the fire and I thought Vincent had too. I bought a fake identity and changed my name and moved to a small town in Pennsylvania. I've been hiding in plain sight until Carter tracked me down, which makes me think that Vincent just let me go."

Her voice broke and she sniffled again.

"Are we completely sure that Carter works for Vincent? I don't know much about Will other than the evening I met him."

Charlotte nodded. "He probably kidnapped me to kill me

but harming you would be the way to get back at him." She paused and although I had several questions running through my mind, I gave her the moment to herself. "He hasn't mentioned Vincent, but I assume that would be the only person who would want to track me down, especially now that I know your connection to Damien." She sniffled again. "Vincent is very thorough and has friends in high places in addition the power that he wields. I assume I'm a loose end and it's only a matter of time before he kills me, especially since I disobeyed his orders. Since Carter hasn't killed either one of us, I assume he's holding out until he can get us to Vincent."

"Does Carter have a schedule for when he comes down here? I assume he brings you food and lets you use the bathroom."

She nodded. "He does, but I couldn't tell you when he comes down."

"That's right, you can't tell because we don't have phones, nor can we see outside... Well, I think we need to have a plan for when he comes for a visit."

NEITHER SHE NOR I knew when Carter was going to come down, but when he did, I pretended to still be out of it. I heard the basement door open with a loud creak and an over-head light turned on. I could see that it lit the room up considerably through my closed eyelids. I wasn't sure where Charlotte had decided to go because she was out of my field of vision, but I had hoped that she had done what she said she was going to do, while I sat in a corner, looking feeble and weak.

"Figure out a way to eat this. We'll be leaving here in a few hours."

I could hear him getting close to me and almost jumped out of my skin when I felt him pull my hair back. He placed his fingers on my neck and mumbled, "Still alive."

I cracked open one eye, glad that my hair was somewhat masking my face and the small vision problem I had earlier was doing better. Just as he was about to place a plate of something in front of me, his body lurched forward. That's when I knew that Charlotte had stuck to the plan.

Charlotte rammed him hard from behind, sending him head-first into the concrete wall, but she didn't stop there. As he fell to the cold stone floor, she kicked him hard in his groin, twice, then stomped on his head, all before he knew what hit him.

It all seemed to happen in slow motion. Once she had him down and hopefully out for a few minutes, she ran over to me, and stood by me, ready to help if she could as I struggled to my feet. I knew I was wasting precious seconds, but my head was still throbbing from that knock on the forehead he'd given me.

Carter groaned as he started to come to, and I knew we needed to get out of there or he'd probably kill us.

"We need to go now!" I rushed with her toward the stairs.

The stairs weren't very steep, but they were difficult to climb with our arms secured behind our backs and my injury. As soon as we reached the top, I kicked the door closed behind us. I took a second to grip the knob and turn the lock. It took me longer than normal with my hands behind my back, but I finally managed it. I wasn't sure if it would hold if he decided to throw his weight against it, but hopefully, it would give us enough time to figure out how to get out of the zip ties.

Glancing about the room we now stood in, we could see that he must have been living up here for a while. There were beer cans and empty pizza boxes littering the coffee table and floor of the living room. Through the doorway, I could see a pile of dishes in the kitchen sink, and an overflowing garbage can that was starting to stink.

"Do you see a weapon or something that we can use to untie our hands?" Charlotte asked.

"We should check the kitchen. Maybe there's a knife or something in there."

We passed through the opening into the small kitchen. It really was tiny, just a sink, fridge, oven, and a small countertop with two drawers and a cabinet below.

"I'll try the drawers." Charlotte backed up toward one of the drawers and used her tied hands to open it.

"Hurry, I think he's on the stairs, Charlotte!" I urged her, but I wasn't sure where he was at the moment. I glanced over my shoulder back toward the living room, praying we'd be faster than Carter.

I moved over toward her and glanced in the drawer, adrenaline pumped through my body and thanked everything I could think of when my eyes landed on a pair of scissors.

"We can use those scissors to cut these off, can you grab them?" I asked. "Never mind. Yank the drawer out, move out of the way, and let the drawer fall. That'll be faster I think."

She did and down went the drawer along with all of its contents.

I winced as we both dropped to the ground and I grabbed the scissors first. Once we were back to back, I used my left hand to feel where her fingers were, I found the small space between her hands where the zip tie held her wrists together. I slipped my fingers into the finger-holes and opened the scissors and just as I made contact with the plastic of the tie, I heard Carter slam his shoulder into the basement door and I jumped, losing my grip on the tie. "Okay, we need to try to line up so that I can cut you free."

"Okay," she said.

It took a little bit more maneuvering than I had planned as Carter's body could be heard ramming into the door again.

"Shit!" I swore, dropping the scissors. Scrabbling, I stretched to pick up the scissors once more. "We're close, just need to line it up properly again."

I stared over my shoulder and almost shouted out when we got Charlotte's binds positioned with the blades of the scissors.

"I think you've got it lined up."

"Okay, it's going to take a bit of chopping because these things are dull. I'm trying not to hurt you."

"Don't worry about that," she said, even though I know she didn't mean it. A pounding on the basement door made her yelp, which caused me to jump.

"Try to ignore him." My breath was coming out in short spurts as Charlotte tried to help by rubbing her hands back and forth against the scissors as I tried to cut the plastic. Of course, the scissors had to be dull because that was just my luck. "Almost got it."

She then yanked on the zip tie. I turned around and looked at her wrists and noticed they were turning red from the strain she was putting on them. When we whittled away another piece of the zip tie, it took one final tug and Charlotte was free.

"Yes!" She didn't even take a moment to nurse her red wrists before she took the scissors out of my hands and began to work on my zip tie.

When we heard the basement door burst open, I yelled, "Oh no! Just go."

"But—"

"Just go!" I screamed, my voice still hoarse. "Take the scissors with you!" I knew there was a slim chance that I would be able to get free if she left the scissors here, but leaving another weapon at Carter's disposal wasn't wise.

Charlotte grabbed the scissors and scrambled to her feet. She ran toward the back door and yanked it open.

"Come back here, you bitch," Carter said. His lips curled into a sneer as he took a step toward her.

"Go!" I yelled at Charlotte. She spared one glance at me before she took off running.

"Well, too bad she left you behind. You're the bigger prize anyway."

8

DAMIEN

All I could think about was probable scenarios that might have happened to Anais and what state she might be in. My mood drifted from rage to sorrow because I was the one who put her in this situation. I tapped my phone, which was resting in the center console, and wondered if now was the right time to call Anais's parents to let them know that their only child was in grave danger. I felt someone clasp their hand around my shoulder, and I turned around and found Broderick leaning forward from his seat in the row behind me.

"Everything is going to be fine. Anais is strong and we're going to get her back."

I wanted to believe that, but there was more going on than just that. It was the feeling that I now knew that the reason she was in this predicament was because of me. I also had no doubt that we would get her back, I just didn't know what shape she would be in when we did.

And that caused the rage in me to build further. Yes, I was furious at Carter, but I was also pissed at myself. I hadn't done enough to protect her and that thought nearly killed me. There was more I could have done. Not knowing whether she was alive or dead caused turmoil to roll through my body.

She's alive. She's going to be okay. As I told myself these words, I wasn't sure if I really believed them. Flashbacks to what happened to Charlotte played in my mind. I remembered how much I had hoped and prayed that by some miracle she had made it out of that burning house alive. When I was at her funeral about a week or so later, guilt surged through me and continued over the years. My feelings for her had turned from sharing times of happiness in the months that we were together to anticipating that her memory would terrorize me once I fell asleep.

I was surprised that by now, Carter hadn't tried to contact either me or Anais's parents demanding conditions of her release. That told me that there was more at play here than we were currently aware.

As the SUV sped down the road, causing the streetlights to be nothing more than a blur, I vowed to make sure I didn't make the same mistakes again.

WE MADE it to New Jersey in record time, but the drive for me had been brutal. Thanks to the lack of traffic on the street and Kingston's superb driving skills, we were now five minutes outside of Gray, New Jersey. It still felt as if we weren't getting there fast enough. Every second that passed meant that her life was on the line, and who knew when Carter might cut the cord?

The thought of losing her made me want to break

through a thousand brick walls. My thoughts came crashing down when Kingston swerved, trying to avoid something that I had missed while I had been caught up in my own head.

"What the fuck?" I said as he swerved to get back on the road and then slammed on the brakes. "Is everyone all right?"

I looked back at my brothers and through the back windshield toward Will's oncoming SUV as it pulled to a stop behind us. Turning forward, I looked to see what Kingston had swerved to miss. A woman ran toward us, waving her arms above her head. My heart stopped, but it soon became apparent that it wasn't Anais.

"What the hell, Kingston!" Broderick yelled from the backseat.

I didn't get a good look at her as she ran over to the driver's side window.

"Please help," she said, trying to catch her breath. She held her hand out, pointing down the road and said, "Me and another woman were kidnapped, and I was able to get free but she's still with him."

"She must be talking about Anais!" My heart pounded in my chest as I tried to undo the seat belt, but my hands were shaking as rage filled me. I was going to kill the fucker if he had hurt one beautiful strand of hair on her head. As I got free of the belt, I pulled my gun and opened the door. The woman couldn't have been running for long. I would find where the fucker was keeping Anais and then I would beat the shit out of him.

I followed where the woman had pointed down the road, and a couple of minutes later, I came across a narrow dirt road that showed footprints from where the woman had been running. I followed it to a cabin that was surrounded by trees.

Had she not pointed it out, I doubted we would have found it so easily.

The cabin looked a bit run-down, but someone was in the process of fixing it up based on the tools located outside. There was a light on the main level, and I hoped, given that it looked to be a relatively small home, it might be easy to locate Anais. Unless he moved her when that woman ran off. I took the safety off my gun and decided to take a look around the cabin. Silently, I moved through the trees, checking it out. When I reached the back, I could see the door was standing open. I headed toward it, quietly so I wouldn't draw Carter's attention. Thankfully, the stairs of the porch didn't shift or make too much noise under my weight. I looked through the kitchen window to see if I could see him or anything that would tell me what I was walking into.

A quick look showed me Carter was standing in the kitchen and I quickly ducked down. If I went in the open back door, he'd be right there, and I wanted to take him by surprise. I moved back down the stairs and went around to the front of the house. If the front door was locked, I wouldn't have a choice but to use the back door, but it was worth it to take him by surprise.

I grabbed the knob and twisted and thankfully it opened quietly. I took a step through the door and closed my eyes for a split second when the floor groaned under my weight. I took a step through the door and closed my eyes for a split second when the floor groaned under my weight. I paused for a moment to see if anyone had been alerted to my arrival. No one came so I stepped farther inside and looked to my left and to my right.

Carter was standing in front of the kitchen counter with Anais at his feet.

Fuck! How did I not see her on the floor when I looked through the window?

The stars had aligned because Carter's back was to me, but Anais's back was up against the cabinets with her head limp, chin on her chest.

I thought I knew what fear was when I hadn't known her fate, but when I saw her like that and she didn't move immediately, real, terrifying fear slammed into me making it hard to breathe. I couldn't tell if she was alive. My heart clenched and I saw nothing but red.

Another second passed and I heard Carter murmuring to himself, yet he didn't look over to the door. Then something drew my attention, a movement, and my eyes were drawn back to Anais, and found her staring back at me. She was alive. The fear left me, but the rage intensified as I watched her eyes widen. I put a finger to my lips to let her know not to alert Carter as I slowly moved toward them.

But something must have given me away, some slight sound or creak of the floor, because suddenly Carter turned around, whipping what looked to be a weapon out toward me. I acted on instinct and shot him in the arm holding the weapon. His knife fell to the ground with a clack and Carter moaned in pain. I kicked the knife further away and dragged him from the kitchen by his hair, closer to the front door.

Carter grunted, but I didn't care that I was hurting the fucker. He didn't know what pain was, but he would by the time I was done with him. For now, I slammed the butt of my gun into his head and knocked him out, letting him drop to the floor. He'd be out for a while, at least long enough for

Kingston to arrive and cart him off. I dashed over to Anais and dropped to my knees in front of her, setting my weapon down at my side within easy reach.

"I'm so glad to see you," she said. Her voice was hoarse and sounded like music to my ears.

"The feeling is mutual."

"Can you...untie me?" I leaned over and saw that her hands were tied behind her back with a zip tie that had scuff marks as if someone had tried to cut it open. I noted that this time around, her wrists weren't as bruised as they were when I tried to save her from sharing the same fate as her father. When I thought about how Carter had done that too, rage filled me once again.

"Did you find—"

Her words were cut off when Kingston came rushing into the cabin with his gun drawn. He surveyed the scene before he walked up to Carter and said, "You have a lot of explaining do, asshole." He turned to us. "Are you two all right?"

"Yeah, we're fine. Do we have a knife in the car? I don't want to use Carter's weapon of choice."

"We might. We definitely have something to cut that with in my bag."

"Sounds good." I stood up and put my gun away but didn't take my eyes off of Anais. I couldn't believe that we found her, and she seemed relatively unharmed. The fear that had a chokehold over me earlier was fading away and relief was taking its place. I bent down to pick up Anais, cradling her as if she were a doll made of glass, and carried her outside.

"I'm so glad to see you," she said.

"You said that already."

"It bears repeating."

I snorted. "That I understand, Spitfire." I looked down at her and noticed a glassy look in her eyes. "You're going to see a doctor."

"Not going to argue with you. My head is throbbing and my body hurts."

"Rest for now. I'm taking care of everything."

"Okay."

With each step I took toward the SUVs parked on a dirt road leading to the cabin, the further away we moved from how quickly I came to losing her.

We were about halfway to the SUV when another one drove up. There were no lights on or sirens blaring so I assumed it wasn't the authorities.

"There's my team," Kingston said from behind me. I glanced over my shoulder and found him walking out of the cabin with Carter, who was still moaning in pain. "Shut up."

"Ow."

"We'll get him back to the warehouse and interrogate him, you'll want to be there, I assume?" At my nod, Kingston glanced over at Will's SUV. "When we get everything settled, you're going to want to hear the rest of the story."

I didn't reply; my attention was focused on making sure that Anais was safely in our SUV. Broderick was in the driver's seat and Gage was sitting in the front seat staring out the windshield like a deer in headlights. I rushed past the driver's side door and opened the back door.

"Damien—wait."

I froze. Those two words sent an ice-cold shiver down my spine. The voice couldn't be real. It was impossible because that voice belonged to someone that I knew was long dead.

My heartbeat slowed and I slowly turned around as two people came toward me. Will I recognized immediately, but the other... the other had to be an apparition because I'd watched her die in a house fire. She looked different now, different hair color, older, but still there was no mistaking her.

"Charlotte?" Her name came out in a harsh whisper as I stared at her.

The trance that Charlotte had over me for a brief moment was broken when Anais moaned in my arms. I needed to make sure that she was okay because she was my priority now. I turned back to the SUV. "Broderick, can you call a doctor or nurse? Have them meet us at the penthouse."

"You got it. I know just who to call."

My eyes drifted back to Charlotte, who was definitely not a ghost or a figment of my imagination.

"Is everything cool with us now?" My gaze didn't shift from Charlotte, but it was Will who spoke.

"You're not going to believe this, but Charlotte is pretty sure our older brother, Vincent, is behind this."

9
_____

ANAIS

"Damien?" My voice sounded rough to my own ears.

"I'm here." He sounded nearby, but I couldn't tell how close.

Determination forced me to open my eyes. I squinted as my eyes tried to adjust. I found Damien sitting in a chair a couple of feet away, with his head in his hands.

"Are you okay?"

Damien looked up at my question and walked over and sat down next to me on the bed. I shifted over slightly to give him more room but winced.

"Don't move."

"I won't do it again because it hurt."

"Grace should be here soon, but you can rest until she gets here."

I stopped myself from nodding my head, instead taking a moment to look at Damien. The soft light from the lamp on the bedside table cast a warm glow in the room. Damien brought me into the bedroom that had once been his but was now ours.

The light also revealed just how much tonight had taken a toll on Damien. From his wrinkled clothes, his hair sticking up in every direction, and the redness that could be found in his gaze.

"I could have lost you tonight."

His voice stopped me from observing his appearance and when I looked up at him, I couldn't stop the wetness that was forming in the corners of my eyes. The slight quiver as he said the words was almost my undoing.

How close I had been to death tonight could be anyone's guess. What I did know was that everything that transpired tonight would stay with me for the rest of life.

"I'm not going to let another moment go by without telling you that I love you."

His words would also stay with me for eternity and beyond. The tears fell from my eyes as I whispered, "I love you too."

His head slowly moved down toward mine, his eyes focusing on my lips. "I'm worried about pulling you into my arms, since we don't know what your injuries are yet. But there is one thing I can do."

His lips came to rest on mine.

～

"Ms. Monroe?"

I could hear someone calling, but I didn't want to wake up. My eyelids felt heavier than I could ever remember them feeling.

"Ms. Monroe?"

The voice was a bit louder, and I tried harder to open my

eyes. Once I was able to open them into tiny slits, I could see a sliver of my surroundings. I couldn't get a good visual of where I was, but I knew there were a few people in the room based on the murmurs I heard in the background. I blinked hard. That seemed to work because I was able to open my eyes wider and catch a glimpse of what was going on in the room. I found myself in our bedroom in the penthouse.

"Hi," I said, my voice barely above a whisper. Someone rushed to my side and when I looked up, I found Damien.

"Anais, how are you feeling?"

"Mostly tired. Head still hurts but I'll take that over the somewhat blurry vision I experienced in the cabin and my body is sore." Tears welled up in my eyes as I relived my experiences over the last twenty-four hours. Who knew what Carter would have done once he moved Charlotte and me? I wondered what happened to her.

Damien grabbed my hand, and I took the opportunity to glance around the room and I found Damien, Broderick, and a blonde woman who I had never met before. When my eyes landed on her, she spoke.

"Hi, I'm Grace. I'm going to take a look at you to see how things are going. We want to make sure you don't need to go to the hospital."

I froze at the word *hospital* and Damien must have felt me tense up. "She's not going to the hospital," he said.

"She will if it means saving her life. Concussions can be tricky. If everything checks out, I'll be happy for her to stay here and you can let me know if she develops any more symptoms. If her symptoms get worse, you need to rush to the emergency room."

Damien didn't have a response. Broderick walked up and

put a hand on Grace's shoulder and said, "Damien, you know she's right. You asked me to call a doctor or a nurse and I called the best doctor I knew." Grace and Broderick glanced at each other before looking back at me. *What's up with them?*

"Let me examine her and I'll let you know what I think."

Damien moved out of the way, allowing Grace to move closer to me. Broderick stepped out of the room, but Damien refused, instead deciding to sit in as Grace started her assessment.

The examination didn't take too long, and Grace took a small step back and said, "So far it looks like Anais is doing as well as could be expected so she can stay here. For the next twenty-four hours, you'll need to make sure she doesn't sleep more than a few hours at a time. No television, phone, or laptop for at least a week, I'd prefer two, but I understand you may need to use your phone and laptop for work, so I'll suggest keeping it to no more than an hour a day. I'll come back and check on her in a few days to make sure that she is improving. Resting is key here." Grace looked at me and then back at Damien. "If you notice anything like vomiting, slurred speech, or if a severe headache isn't getting better let me know and bring her into the emergency room. Sometimes symptoms of a concussion don't show for a few days."

Damien nodded. "Thanks for coming."

"It wasn't any trouble. Happy to help."

Grace turned her attention to the door and opened it. Broderick appeared and asked, "Is everything okay?"

Grace nodded.

"Good. Are you still coming over with Hunter to get pizza and watch basketball on Sunday?"

"Since I'm off, I wouldn't miss it."

"Let me walk you out." With that Broderick and Grace left the room.

"What was that—"

"Anais, don't worry about it. We need to focus on you getting well."

"But what about Charlotte?"

Damien's eyes froze over. "She's okay. We can talk more about that later."

GROGGINESS FLOATED over me like a heavy blanket as I tried to wake up the next morning. I vaguely remembered being woken up multiple times last night by Damien. I groaned as I started to feel my muscles working again. Flashbacks of the events at the cabin slammed into me. I thought I had been lucky enough to escape them while I was dreaming, but it seemed my luck ran out as the weight of those memories crushed me while I was awake. Parts of last night were a blur. The feeling that I was going to die in that basement was very much real. I had wondered if I would ever see my parents or Ellie again.

I heard a noise come from another corner of the room and I turned my head slightly. I found Damien typing on his computer in a comfortable-looking black chair that was closest to the side of the bed that I was lying on. I'd worried about not seeing him again either.

The images of the chaos when Charlotte and I tried to escape and when she finally did flooded back to the surface. I wondered where Charlotte was as I moved again, trying to get comfortable and ease the thoughts of the trauma I had experienced over the last twenty-four hours out of my brain.

Damien either heard me or saw me move because he looked over. He placed the laptop at his feet and came over to me, still the picture of perfection and control.

"Hey, how are you doing?"

"Better. I think." I moved to sit up in bed. My voice sounded better, and my headache had lessened, showing me that I was healing from this ordeal. At least, physically.

"Don't move too much. Doctor's orders." Damien placed a firm hand on my shoulder, slowing my pace before moving to fluff my pillows and then helping me sit up.

"So, this gives you even more reason to be bossy."

"When have I ever needed an excuse?"

That made me snort. He sat down next to me on the bed and tucked a piece of my hair behind my ear. The soft gesture sent a warmth through my body that I hadn't felt since Damien lifted me out of the disaster area that had been the cabin. Now that I was more lucid, there were questions that I wanted answered that I was tired of avoiding.

"What's going to happen to Carter?"

"Don't worry about him. He will be taken care of."

I chose my next words wisely because I knew that it was opening another can of worms. "Then I assume you talked to Charlotte. She's fine, right?"

He stiffened at the mention of her. I was hesitant to ask about her again, but she was an integral part of what was going on. "She's going to be fine. You were by far in worse condition than she was. She's under Will's protection now. Kingston offered a couple of his men, but Will declined."

"How many people work for Kingston?" I blurted the question out and left Damien chuckling.

"I'm not sure, but he has a whole operation that he has built from the ground up. Tried to recruit Broderick, Gage, and me, but we decided to offer funds for the initial investment instead. The rest is history."

"And as far as we know, Carter was the only one who slipped through the cracks? I don't want Charlotte to be harmed."

"Yes. Kingston's team has been working day and night to make sure that Carter was the only rogue team member and so far, that is looking to be the case. You seem to be pretty attached to Charlotte's well-being."

"I am." I took in a deep breath before I continued. "She saved my life."

"I know, and for that, I will forever be grateful."

"I think it would be wise if you two spoke as well." Based on what she told me, I thought her words might help ease some of the pain that Damien had been dealing with years after the fire.

"That is not up for discussion."

I wasn't shocked by his words. I was shocked that he let this conversation continue for as long as it had. I couldn't stop the yawn that passed my lips.

"You are overexerting yourself."

"No I'm not. I'm not doing anything but talking."

Damien gave me a pointed glare.

"Well, it seems that we know that chances are that Charlotte's brother is the one behind all of this."

Damien nodded. "That hasn't been confirmed, but we'll find out more information about that soon. Charlotte mentioned something about it to Broderick and Gage when she confirmed her identity."

His words had a strong whiff of danger and apprehension. He let his brothers handle the woman whose memory had haunted him for years instead of doing it himself. I assumed part of that was due to him taking care of me, but I wondered if he was avoiding her on purpose. I wanted to tell him that I thought it was important that they spoke, but I didn't want to push him any further.

"How long have I been out?"

"Well, it's about 3:00 p.m."

That meant I had been sleeping on and off for about eight hours.

"Have you been waking me up every couple of hours?"

Damien nodded. That meant that he hadn't been able to rest much at all either. "You should get some more rest."

"I think a bath might help relax me and make it more likely that I'd fall asleep." I also wanted to take the opportunity to remove the grime as well.

Damien stood up. "We can make that work. I'll go run a bath."

"Thank you."

It felt weird to have him wait on me, but I didn't read too much into that. I slowly took the covers off of me in an abundance of caution, because I didn't know how my body would feel or how well I could currently move due to the concussion or any sore muscles and bruises I had.

"Hey, don't move too fast," Damien said as he walked out of the bathroom and spotted the position that I was in. He helped me up and took me to the bathroom where I saw myself in the mirror for the first time.

"Well, I look horrible." The bruising on my forehead said as much and I tried to mentally prepare myself for what I would find once I rid myself of all of my clothes.

Damien sat me down on the edge of the tub before he responded. "You are and always will be beautiful. The most beautiful and elegant person that has ever entered my life. Inside and out. And the people that did this to you will now answer to me."

The finality in his words was what made me stay quiet and I turned my attention to the tub that was quickly filling up with warm water. When it was at the perfect depth, Damien reached over and turned it off.

"You know, I didn't even realize you changed my clothes." He had put me in some of his clothes that were a loose fit on me.

"I knew the clothes that you had on weren't going to be comfortable for you to rest in. How much help do you need?"

"Thank you. I can definitely get my shirt off, but the pants might be a little difficult," I said, making moves to taking my shirt off. That was when a memory clicked. "Oh my God. I didn't tell you that I think either Carter stole the engagement ring, or it got lost when he was bringing me to the cabin."

"Don't worry about it."

"It seems to me there are a whole lot of things I shouldn't be worried about that I'm actually worrying about."

"You hated it anyway."

I was speechless, but what he said was true. The ring wasn't what I had envisioned, and I was upset that I didn't have any input in its selection even if it was for a fake engagement. I decided to focus on getting in the tub. It took longer than normal for me to take my clothes off, but it hadn't been as a result of me staring at the bruises that had formed on my body.

Damien's eyes lingered on my naked body before he spoke.

"I didn't see all of these last night," he murmured before helping to lower me into the tub. After he did that, he walked toward the door and dimmed the lights so that there was a nice warm glow.

"Where are you going?"

"To change the bedsheets. I'll come back in soon to bring you back to bed."

"You aren't going to have someone come over and do it for you?"

Damien bent down on one knee and smirked at me. "You don't think I know how to change the sheets on a bed?"

"I—uh."

"It keeps me humble." He didn't say anything else before he left, and I found myself laughing. It felt good to laugh out loud.

I don't know how long I soaked in the tub, but a soft knock brought me out of the daydream I was in. Had this been the first time Damien ever knocked before entering a room I was in? "Come in."

Damien strolled into the room. "Are you done with your bath?"

"I am."

Damien helped me stand up before grabbing a towel off of the warming rack and wrapping me up in it. He stood by me as I walked back into his bedroom and found a freshly made bed, some of my cosmetics, and another set of Damien's sweatpants and a T-shirt that I didn't even know he had. I could have cried from happiness, but I swallowed those tears.

"Thank you," I whispered as I sat down on the bed.

As I got ready for bed, Damien said, "Your parents and Ellie are on their way back to New York City to be with you."

"That's great. I miss them."

"I know you do."

"I'm starting to feel a little more tired."

"That's fine. Go to sleep and then when you wake up, they will be here."

He helped me get into bed and I mumbled something in agreement, but I couldn't even remember what I said. My mind drifted to sweet dreams that I hoped wouldn't be interrupted by the nightmare I had just lived.

THE NEXT TIME I woke up, I heard chattering in the living room. It was dark outside, making it harder to recognize what time it was, but I assumed it was the evening of the same day. It took a few moments for me to will myself to reach over to turn on the lamp on the bedside table near me.

It was there that I found my purse and grabbed it off the bedside table. I looked to see if all my things were inside. When I picked up my phone, I heard a light knock on the door.

"Come in," I said, feeling weird telling someone to come into Damien's bedroom. Speaking of Damien, he was the one who had knocked and greeted me with a small smile.

"Did you sleep well?"

"I think so. Are my parents and Ellie here?"

Damien nodded. "And they'll be staying in the building for a little while to be closer to you."

That brought a smile to my face. "Yes! I want to go see them," I said as I whipped off the covers.

"How about they come in here?"

"But you don't like people being in your bedroom."

He shrugged. "Some things change." He wasn't wrong about that either. "I'll bring them in here and then I'll have to head out. There are guards at the door making sure that no one enters or leaves without my permission."

"Where are you going?" I asked.

"I have some business to take care of, but it shouldn't take too long."

I started to ask what he meant but stopped myself when I heard my mom say Damien's name. Damien turned around and waved them in and soon my parents and Ellie came rushing over to me.

"Oh, my baby," Mom said as she softly pulled me into my arms. "My baby. How are you feeling?"

"Hi, Mom. I'm doing better."

Dad came over and although he looked better, I could see that he still looked worse for wear. My eyes bounced between my parents and realized that neither one of them had slept much since I assume Damien had told them I had been injured. Now, how much he had told them was up for debate and I knew I had to be careful what I said.

Ellie sat down at the foot of the bed and gave me a small smile. It felt great to see her again too. Damien pulled up two black chairs that he kept in the sitting area of his room up to the bed, giving my parents a place to sit.

They both did and Dad looked up at Damien before

sticking his hand out. "Thank you for saving my daughter's life."

When Damien reached out and shook his hand in return, I could see the mutual understanding passing between the two.

"Anais—" Mom was ready to rapidly fire off some questions, but Dad turned and placed a hand on her knee.

"Don't give Anais the third degree just yet. I'm sure she's exhausted from everything that happened."

I knew how hard it was for Mom not to say anything and my gaze floated to Damien, who was making his way out the room.

"Damien, be careful out there."

He responded without turning around. "I always am."

10

DAMIEN

"I can't wait to get my hands on that fucker," I said as I sped down the street.

I glanced over at Kingston, who was busy on his phone doing who knows what. Broderick was sitting quietly in the back but Gage said something had come up, although he had wanted to join in on the "fun" that was going to be had. Kingston's team came in and cleared Carter's apartment and the cabin he kept in New Jersey with ease over the course of the last day and a half or so.

I asked Will if he wanted to join, but he left what was going to happen to Carter up to me. I had hoped to talk to Charlotte before I saw Carter again, but she was still recovering. I also needed to talk to Will about Vincent, whom I'd never met or seen before, but his main priority was tending to his sister.

"Couldn't we get Rob to drive? Driving a little wild over there."

I glared at Broderick through the rear-view mirror, who in turn smirked. "I felt like driving tonight. Be happy that I haven't thrown your ass in the river." I turned my attention to Kingston. "Did your guys find anything at his place or in the cabin? Maybe something pointing to Vincent?"

"Still looking through everything, but so far no. It might be easier to force him to talk when we get there."

The desire to show Carter that he didn't fuck with what was mine would be rectified momentarily. I tightened my hands. "Did you find anything about where Vincent is?"

Kingston shook his head. "No one knows where he is. All signs point to him skipping town although we both know he didn't." He cleared his throat. "Is everything okay with you?"

"Why?"

"You make it a point of always maintaining control, yet I can feel you about to spin out of control on this one. You're holding on to the steering wheel so tight, that I wouldn't be surprised if it cracked under the pressure."

I glanced at him, feeling the tension building in the car. "I'm still in control."

"You just had to rescue the woman you love after she was kidnapped and then found out that the girlfriend you thought was dead is anything but. That would fuck anyone up."

"Love?"

I saw Kingston look up from his phone out of the corner of my eye.

"Anyone can see it. You're not doing a good job of hiding it. It's either that or you're getting soft."

"He's right." And there was Broderick chiming in from the back.

"We are not going to talk about this now or ever."

Broderick grunted, but it was too late. He was already in my crosshairs.

"Don't you have enough things to worry about? Especially when it comes to a certain doctor that we all know?"

"Shut up, man," he said.

"Got him," Kingston said. The unexpected comment forced us all to chuckle, a much-needed change from the dark mood that had taken over the SUV since we started our journey.

Once more silence overtook the vehicle as I headed toward an abandoned warehouse in Staten Island. A low fog covered the streets as we drove along with the GPS guiding us to our destination. The closer we got to the warehouse the more abandoned the streets surrounding it were. The number of people and cars in the area decreased the farther we went until my GPS told me that the building was up ahead. I parked the SUV in front of a warehouse that looked to be deserted on the outside, but that was done by design.

We stepped out of the car and went to a huge building with graffiti on it. There was a dull light shining through one of the windows, but other than that it looked as if there was no one around. The perfect place to carry out the activities that were about to take place.

Kingston walked up to the building first and knocked on the door before establishing who we were. When the door opened, it confirmed what I knew all along: what was occurring inside this warehouse was a completely different animal. Inside, the building was buzzing with activity. The warehouse was bigger than I realized on the inside and was designed like a high-tech office filled to the brim with computers. A quick estimation told me that there were about twice as many computers as there were people. For those members of the team who didn't come into the office full-time, maybe? We trusted Kingston with how he ran his business, but I didn't realize he was doing all of this.

One man walked over and shook Kingston's hand and pointed to a door on the right. "Down there."

Kingston opened a door and a set of stairs greeted us. How ironic was it that Carter had been thrown into a basement as well? Rage and adrenaline pumped through me as Kingston, Broderick, and I descended the stairs, and I couldn't help but smirk at the sight before me. There sat Carter, in the middle of a room with a couple of bright lights illuminating the place. His arms were tied behind his back. A couple of men were standing several yards behind him and I knew they were ready to finish Carter if he tried anything.

"About time you bastards turned on the lights in here."

"Good evening, Carter. Doesn't feel great being stuck in a room in total darkness, does it?" Kingston said as he approached the man in the chair. His dirty, bloody, gray shirt was ripped at the sleeve to make room for the bandage that was wrapped around his arm. Satisfaction surged through me at seeing the wound that I caused. I hoped it hurt like a son of a bitch. I was happy that he looked like shit, but he should be pleased he was alive.

"Fuck you," he said.

"That's not how you should talk to the person who holds your life in their hands, is it? Where is Vincent?" I didn't recognize my own voice as the sinister words hung in the air.

"I don't know who the hell you are talking about," he said.

His eyes darted between Kingston, Broderick, and me told me that either he was worried about what would happen to him or he was lying. I decided that it was both and I walked up to him with my fists clenched. I gave him a small smirk before I threw the first punch. The crunch of bones under my hand made the sting of impact worth it. This was gratifying, more so than when I killed Jon. Why had I stopped taking care of these types of things and let Kingston's squad handle them?

He laughed as blood poured from his mouth. "I bet you wouldn't do that if I had my hands untied, bastard. No way you could've done that had we been on equal ground."

I snorted because I knew he was full of shit. "Now where is Vincent?"

This time Kingston joined in on the fun and threw another punch. That one led to one of Carter's teeth flying out of his mouth. Then, he spit out another.

"I loosened it for you," I said.

Kingston gave me a sarcastic chuckle and I glanced at Broderick, who was now rolling up his sleeves, clearly preparing to jump in at any moment.

"Tell us where Vincent is."

"You're all fucking insane."

"That's the sincerest compliment you could have ever given us," I said as I took a step to my left and squeezed the arm where I shot Carter. His scream of pain was elevated once more when Broderick got in on the action. But still he said nothing.

I released his arm from my grasp. Kingston strolled over to me and out of the corner of my eye, I saw him reach out his hand. I opened mine and he placed a pistol in it. I checked the gun before I took a step back, held it up, and aimed and yet there was no response from him. A smirk appeared on my face just before I shot him in the foot.

"Ah! Okay! Okay! Fuck, I'll talk, you sick son of a bitch. I'll tell you what I know if it stops you assholes from beating on me." His words came out muffled due to the damage we inflicted on him.

I took a step back and shrugged, dropping my arms to my sides. "Fine. Spill."

"I don't know where Vincent is. I swear. All of our transactions took place either over burner phones or in public spaces."

"When was the last time you saw him?"

Carter swallowed hard. "The night Anais snuck out and went to Hidden Tavern. I was standing outside when she left the penthouse's garage. I alerted Vincent, who staged everything else at Hidden Tavern. It was one of his hangouts."

And this was why Dave, the private investigator who worked for Cross Industries, was one of the best in the business. If he'd had a little more time to put two and two together...

"It was happenstance that I ended up working for Vincent. He put out feelers for someone to join him on this job just as I was getting my feet wet at Cross Sentinel, but I don't know how long he was tracking you all. The plan was to hurt you the way your father hurt his, and to kidnap his sister, whom he knew was alive the entire time, and bring her back here to face what he viewed as treacherous behavior. He was still pissed that she hadn't done what she was supposed to do when it came to killing you and he wanted her to pay."

"So, you've been tracking me for years."

Carter nodded. "And who knows how long Vincent has

been but if there was one thing that I learned about working with him is that he's patient. So, while you think you've won since you've captured me, you are highly mistaken. Vincent is still walking these streets and will wait to strike."

I thought it was funny how he thought he was still in any position to threaten me, but I continued my questioning. "How did Anais get pulled into this?"

"She fell into this because of the deal you struck with her father." Carter paused to spit out some more blood. "We started tracking anyone that you did business with and it wasn't hard to guess that if you caught sight of her, you would have wanted to claim her. I mean, who wouldn't?"

Broderick's arm stopped me from fucking Carter's face up more before I could think to move on him.

"Once we confirmed your intentions the rest was easy because I was already on the inside. My job was just to deliver Anais and Charlotte to him. I didn't know what he planned on doing with them once I delivered them because that was the end of my job. At first, he wanted me to hold out because he assumed you didn't care about her just like the other women you slept with, but that turned out to be false. When Anais stuck around and lasted longer than the rest, we started planning our move and when you guys broke up, I was placed on her security detail. And then the shooting brought you two back together, closer than ever."

I hated to admit that I believed him. I took a step forward, refusing to look at Kingston or Broderick because I knew they would have smug looks on their faces, but I addressed Kingston first, although I was staring at Carter. "We need to find everything on Vincent as soon as possible."

"Already on it."

"Tell me this, why did you leave that note from Charlotte?"

"To fuck with you. I actually came up with that idea myself to cause you to spin out of control. We knew there was no way you could have moved on from that night unscathed."

"But it failed because—"

Carter interrupted me, "You know what we couldn't figure out though? We couldn't figure out why Anais was different from the other women that floated in and out of your life. I mean other than being smoking hot—"

He stopped because I took a step forward and bent down to look Carter right in the face. "You have a death wish and I'm happy to grant it."

"Either you're going to kill me, or Vincent is. There's no way that I'm making it out of this alive. I didn't deliver the women in the timeframe he wanted. I'm as good as dead, but so are you."

"You think that Vincent is going to avenge your death? Laughable. I'm glad you came to the same realization that you're a dead man no matter what."

"Whoa." Carter's deer-in-headlights look was the first real emotion he had shown all night outside of when pain was inflicted on him.

"You thought I was going to give Vincent the pleasure of killing you? After all you did to what is mine?" I scoffed. "I only agreed to stop beating on you. Thanks for all of the information."

Carter shook briefly before his expression turned stoic, accepting his fate. All of this could have been avoided if he had done the right thing by not taking the job of Vincent's lackey. Or even if he would've told Kingston the plan, he might've saved his own life. I could let Kingston's men take over, but where would the fun be in that? He needed to pay for the turmoil he had inflicted on Anais and her family. I made a promise to myself to protect her at all costs, and this was the first step into rectifying it.

He tangled with the devil and it was time to pay the price. I pulled the trigger, finally feeling satisfied.

11

ANAIS

I was still awake when Damien returned, and I smiled at him when he walked through the front door. My parents and Ellie left about thirty minutes ago after I had made my way to the living room to turn on some music in an effort to take my mind off of everything.

"Everything all right?" I carefully looked him over. He didn't seem to be bleeding anywhere. Or so I thought until I noticed his right hand. "Let me see it," I said as he walked closer to me on the couch.

"You should be in bed."

"Yes, I know, but I'm resting by sitting on the couch. And no, I didn't walk here by myself, Ellie helped me get settled here. By the way, thank you for renting out a couple of apartments in the building for them to stay in the short term."

"They help you and you care about them, so I'm making sure they are nearby. It also helps with security concerns. Did Lucy come by with meals?"

"She did. I had one of the dinners she left, and it was delicious. I know you're attempting to change the subject."

I thought I was the one who always tried to deflect. The closer he came to me, the more I could feel the energy leaping off of him. His hand slightly shook before he put it down at his side. Damien removed his coat and tossed it over the back of the chair. Had I ever seen him not keep things neat?

"Everything is fine. Things have been taken care of or are in the process of being taken care of."

"Where is Carter now?"

"Somewhere he won't bother you again."

I reached over and grabbed Damien's uninjured hand. "Stop trying to shield me from this. Where is Carter?"

My tone was unwavering, and I deserved to know an answer. Damien raked a hand through his hair before he looked at me. When our eyes connected, I could still see the fury in his. "He's in hell, which is where he belongs for hurting you both physically and emotionally. He gave us some information that helped fill in some gaps, but not all of them."

That confirms that Jon and Carter are both dead and I couldn't give a damn. Fuck them. Damien's hand clenched the back of the couch, his knuckles turning white, and I sighed. "What else aren't you telling me, Damien?"

"You're safer than you were with Carter on the loose, but the person who hired him is still out there."

"Raspy-voice man. Vincent DePalma, I mean. How could I forget his name?"

Damien picked up my hand and started rubbing small circles into my palm. "The quicker we find him, the better. He also has a lot to answer for. Along with my father."

That led to a double take. "What does your father have to do with this?"

"Vincent is doing all of this to avenge his father's death, which he thinks my father was involved in. Now, we need to get the bottom of this. And the quicker we do, the better."

"Damien." He looked at me and said nothing, waiting for me to continue. Thoughts were swirling through my mind about telling him how much I missed him while he was gone, even with my family here, but I cleared my throat and said, "Definitely. I understand that."

"You know what else I think you'll also understand?"

"What's that?"

"That once you're fully healed, I'm going to put you over my knee and spank that ass until it's a pretty pink color and then I'm going to take you from behind, which I know we will both enjoy."

I let him change the subject this time because he instilled his trust in me. It was the first time that I felt as if he viewed me as a partner versus another person who he could just tell what to do. He wasn't wrong about that. I would never tell him this, but I missed being with him. Our relationship hadn't started off on the right foot, but I looked forward to us connecting with one another in multiple ways in the bedroom and outside of it.

"Damien, come to bed so you can finally get some rest."

"Are you now giving the orders around here?"

"Looks like it."

I WAS RUNNING toward the light; my salvation seemed to be in reach. My arms and legs propelled my body forward and I could see that I was getting closer and closer. That was until hands grabbed at me, pulling me in the opposite direction. I refused to be deterred and fought against the forces that were trying to yank me toward the darkness. I wasn't going back there.

It seemed the more I struggled, the harder it was to move, but I knew this couldn't stop me. It wouldn't stop me.

That was until I heard a gunshot. The loud blast made me stop moving and consequently, the hands that were holding me back fell by the wayside. Why had they let go?

I looked behind me but saw nothing but darkness. My gaze drifted around me until it landed on my stomach where I found blood seeping through the white T-shirt that I hadn't realized I was wearing. Panic surged through my veins as I placed my hands on the hole in my abdomen. The pressure that I was applying on the wound wasn't doing anything because blood slipped through my fingers. I looked up and found someone running toward me just as I dropped to my knees, feeling light-headed and losing energy from blood loss and from having fought against what was holding me back.

A shadowy figure appeared in the light up ahead and the person took off running toward me. As I was falling to the ground, I saw Damien's face appear before me.

I woke up with tears in my eyes, looking around the cool, dark room. I felt my chest before my hands ended up on my cheeks and I tried to calm my racing heart. A glance down at my stomach confirmed that nothing was there but the tank top I had fallen asleep in the night before.

Having a nightmare a few nights after I'd been kidnapped wasn't surprising. While my body aches and concussion symptoms lessen, it seemed as if my fears took over my dreams and turned them into nightmares. I took a moment to take a breath before removing the covers off of my body. I found a sweatshirt that I threw over one of the black chairs in the bedroom. Once I felt some sense of security, I walked toward the bedroom door, hoping to find the person who should have been sleeping beside me.

I opened the door and snuck down the hall where I heard Damien talking to someone in his office with the door opened a smidge.

"Nothing yet?" Damien didn't say anything back right away as he listened to the person on the other end. I waited to see if he would say something else to give me a hint about what he was talking about. Who the hell would he be talking to at this time of night?

I took a step closer to see if maybe I could pick up on anything the other person was saying. Nothing.

"We'll check in tomorrow." When he hung up the phone, I opened his office door and he glanced at me. "You don't ever do what you're supposed to do."

"Shouldn't you be doing the same?"

"Work never sleeps."

"That didn't sound like work."

"It's nothing for you to worry about. Let's get you back to bed." He stood up and walked over to me. "You've been crying. What's wrong?"

"Just had a bad dream. I'm fine."

He pulled me into his arms and a few more tears fell from my eyes. Having someone know what you needed before you realize it was life changing for me. To have someone know you well enough and to love you, faults and all, was a magical experience. I appreciated him not asking me what happened in the dream right now because I was afraid to relive it.

"You know there's another way that we can take your mind off of that nightmare."

His words opened up something inside of me that told me I was ready for whatever he had planned. He helped me remove my sweatshirt and I knew that without a doubt, I was in for a pleasurable ride.

"Oh, really?" My voice came out as a breathless whisper. The heat in his eyes gave me a hint as to what he was referring to. "Finally going on a date to Thirteen Park Avenue? I'm still waiting on that by the way."

Damien chuckled. "No. This would be...closer to home. Much closer."

Him calling this place our home made my heart swell. "What did you have in mind?"

The light in his eyes darkened before his lips descended onto mine. The touch of his lips was almost my undoing. I felt as if it had been so long since the last time we kissed with such heat and passion. I knew that he was treating me like a delicate flower after Carter kidnapped me, and I was happy to see that the passion and desire had been building up inside of him just like it had been in me. It was time to unleash all of this pent-up energy.

"You don't know how fond I am of you wearing these cute skimpy pajamas to bed." He left small kisses on my lips after every third word.

"No, you never mentioned it."

"That was my mistake. It's time to rectify that."

I reached for his pajama pants, but he stopped me. "Not tonight, Spitfire. This was just for you. Sit down."

His words made my hands stop midair. Curious about what he had planned, I sat down on the couch, my body shivering at the sharp contrast between my hot skin and the coolness of the leather cushion. Damien followed suit and before I could blink, his lips were on mine. His kisses started out soft before they became hungrier, as if he needed to get closer to me than he already was.

The kiss turned feverish in its intensity and I didn't know the placement of his hands until they were on my breasts. Heat traveled through my body and landed in the place where I wanted him to pay the most attention to. When he broke our kiss, I longed for him to come back because I wanted to feel the weight of his lips on my own.

Damien slowly made his way from my lips to my jaw to my neck to my chest. He left a trail of light kisses in his wake. He continued lightly massaging my breasts through my tank top and my desire for him continued to grow.

He moved his head and whispered into my ear, "How wet are you for me?"

His breath lightly tickled the shell of my ear and I shuddered. "I'm dripping."

"No surprises there since it's been a while. You know what to do. Spread 'em."

His demand sent another surge through me. Without needing any convincing, I opened my legs, ready to receive whatever he was going to give me. He moved off the couch and kneeled in front of me. I felt like a queen on her throne as I watched through heavy eyes what he was going to do next.

"This pussy is mine."

I nodded my head, not sure if he saw me, and not caring,

to be frank. I didn't trust my mouth to form any words while I eagerly tried to anticipate his next move. His fingertips moved toward my pajama shorts, caressing the fabric of my waistband. I could feel his touch through the pants, but I needed more.

As if he heard my thoughts, he pulled at the fabric. "Lift your bottom."

I did as he asked and soon my shorts and underwear descended down my legs. He tossed them over his shoulder, neither one of us caring where they landed. My body dropped back down onto the cushion and the contrast between the temperature of my skin and the couch felt like a cool reprieve this time. That didn't last long, however.

It wasn't long before Damien was staring at my aching, wet pussy. "Move your bottom forward."

I did as he said, and I felt the light touch of his finger draw up and down my folds.

"You weren't lying."

Before I could say anything, his mouth descended on me and a huge moan left my lips, finally happy to have him where I ached for him most. Who needed food when he was acting as if I was his last meal?

He shifted his body, causing my legs to widen in order to accommodate him, and the extra room must have been what he needed because he began to devour me. The rhythm he was keeping with his tongue was bringing me closer and closer to a peak that I hadn't reached in what felt like forever, and when he added one finger, and then two, I cried out.

"You're getting close."

All I could do was nod my head. I looked down at him and found him looking back at me with such intensity that between having his gaze on me and his fingers stroking me at just the right pace, I came undone, letting out a long-awaited release. The smirk on Damien's face told me that he was pleased with the outcome.

He stood up and placed his middle finger in his mouth, sucking my juices off it before he said, "I just can't get enough of your taste."

I wondered if I could have another orgasm just from his words.

When I caught my breath, I reached for his pants once more before he stepped out of my reach.

"Spitfire, I told you this was strictly for you. If you put your mouth on me, it won't just end there. And I want you at your best when it's time for me to fuck you again."

THE NEXT MORNING, Grace stopped by to check in on me. She performed a brief examination but focused more on asking me questions once she sat down in the black chair, just across from the couch I was lying on.

"I see Damien went back to work. I was surprised to see Kingston standing at the door when I was brought up."

I snorted. "He's been having a couple of in-person meetings here and there, but he should be home in about an hour or so. It feels weird to have him around so often nowadays."

Grace nodded before getting down to business. "How are you doing?"

"Not too bad. A small headache, some tiredness and soreness, but I assume it's my body healing."

"That it is. And it seems that you're getting around better."

That was true. I had opened the door myself to let her in and had been resting on the couch before she arrived.

"Fantastic. Keep an eye on any changes, but you look good to me. I still want you to avoid doing strenuous activities and continue to get as much rest as you can."

Resting might drive me up the wall, but I knew how vital it was to my recovery, so whatever it took. Plus, it wasn't like I couldn't go downstairs and see my parents and Ellie if I wanted to.

"You'll be back up and running in no time, but I repeat, take it easy as much as possible. Based on what I've heard about you, I assume you really want to go back to work."

I was willing to still be out for a couple more days, but once I felt as if I was back to normal, I knew the desire to work would return. "I don't want to overdo it and potentially end up in a worse position."

"That's the right attitude to have. If you need anything, you have my card right there on your bedside table, and Damien knows how to get in touch with me."

I debated with myself about whether or not to ask the thing that had been on the tip of my tongue since I met her. I knew it was somewhat inappropriate but when you have a lot of time to sit back and just think of random things while you're supposed to be resting, it stirs in your brain.

"I can't remember if I told you this before but thank you for coming on such short notice the night of the attack."

Grace smiled at me. "It was my pleasure. Broderick seemed a little panicked when he called me, and I was happy to assist."

There was my opening. "How do you and Broderick know

each other?" I tried to be as vague as possible as a way to not alert her to the fact that I was digging for information.

"Broderick and my brother have been best friends for..." She paused for a moment. "Has it been twenty-five years? Maybe? Sorry, it's hard to keep track."

"That's okay. It happens to me as well. That's a long time."

Grace smiled. "Yeah, he's been annoying me for about that long, but he's a good guy. The number of things I could tell you about him...well, we would be here all day. I've got him out of so much stuff over the years...usually due to Gage or my brother, Hunter, dragging him along."

I chuckled, and based on what I knew of them, this wasn't at all shocking. "I'm sure they both could make life quite entertaining."

"Oh, that's for sure. I'm not so sure how Selena made it with all three of them running her house into the ground. Then adding Hunter or Kingston into the mix and, well, you know what I mean."

I grinned and nodded before I winced slightly, wishing I hadn't moved.

"Are you okay?"

"Yes, just shouldn't have nodded that aggressively." I waved my hand. "Don't worry about me, I'm fine."

"Okay. You need to get more rest, and I'm going to get out of here, but it was nice seeing you and I hope we get to see each other again real soon."

"Thank you so much for everything."

"Not a problem." Grace stood up and shook my hand before leaving the apartment, closing the door behind her.

12

DAMIEN

I was lying in bed watching as Anais slept peacefully beside me. Both of us had forgotten to close the curtains, but now the moonlight provided the perfect lighting and backdrop for me to watch my sleeping beauty. I woke up when my arm fell asleep underneath her head, and although my brain was yelling at me to move, I refused. Lying here beside her, stroking her arm up and down, I resisted the urge to wake her in hopes that she would continue to rest.

I longed to take her body again, but I knew that she was healing from the wounds that had developed both physically and mentally. I replayed the moments that we spent together at Elevate in my mind, but it wasn't just due to the sex being phenomenal. It was because of what our relationship had developed into that made the moments where we enjoyed each other's bodies even more incredible. Our relationship grew so quickly that I knew I would do anything for her, including kill, and I had. I wondered if this was the same feeling that my parents had for one another.

Mine. That was the only thing I could think of when I

looked at her. I had done my part to keep my feelings at bay. To remain unattached in every sense of the word besides a roll in the sack had always been the goal when it came to women. But this was different. She was different. What we had was different. If the time during which she was stolen from me taught me one thing, it was that life was precious, and so was my time with her. It could have all been gone in the blink of an eye if Vincent had gotten the opportunity to have her in his grasp.

I saw the expression on Anais's face when she told me that her engagement ring was missing. What she didn't know was that I was relieved it was gone too. Yes, it had cost a small fortune, but it could be replaced. She couldn't. I knew how much she hated that ring, and the ring represented a lie that we were perpetuating to the world. That was over.

"I'm going to fix all of this," I whispered, a vow only I could hear. A few ideas appeared in my head, but first I needed to have a conversation with my father.

The prickliness in my arm won and I moved one of my limbs to get out from underneath her. I turned to throw my other arm over her waist, molding my body to fit hers. As I was about to doze off back to sleep, I felt Anais shiver against me. It was then that I realized that a thin layer of sweat had broken out on her back.

A low groan escaped her lips. I sat up, but kept my arm on her waist, hoping that it would provide a sense of comfort that could transcend to the dreams I suspected she was having.

"No." Her voice was just above a whisper, the end of the word sounding more like she was moaning in pain.

"Anais," I said low, hoping to wake her up from the

turmoil she was embroiled in. It didn't work and she whipped her body out from underneath my arm, catching me temporarily off guard. She had flipped over onto her back and the jerkiness of her body made me think that she was either trying to fight or run away from someone in her sleep.

"Anais," I said louder. Still she didn't wake up and tossed once more. "Anais," I repeated and gently shook her awake.

I watched as her eyes popped open, yet she wasn't truly with me for another couple of seconds. Her gaze searched the dark room and when they landed on me, she visibly relaxed.

"Damien." That one word seemed to help slow her rapidly beating heart and she turned her body to lean into mine. I hugged her, gently stroking her back in hopes that she wouldn't have too much trouble falling back to sleep.

"Bad dream again?" I asked although I knew the answer. It seemed as if the nightmares that I faced had been transferred to her. And all of this was because of me.

"Yes, I was dreaming that I was running away from Carter. He caught me but I don't know what happened because you woke me up. Thank you."

"It's not a problem. You know I'm always here for you."

She pulled back and wiped the sleep from her eyes and looked back at me before she said, "Looks like we both have demons that we fight when sleep is supposed to come."

"True," I said. "Mine seem to have faded since we found out that Charlotte was alive."

"Yes, and I'm glad. I noticed you weren't waking up in the middle of the night."

"And you're going to make it past this too." I pulled her into my arms again and brushed my fingers through her hair. I heard her sigh softly and I hoped that was a sign that the terror she had faced in her dreams would become dormant once again so that she could fall back to sleep.

"I know."

"DAMIEN! Did I miss Melissa calling to schedule a meeting with Mr. Cross?"

"You didn't." The next morning, I showed up to Dad's office unannounced on purpose. I didn't tell him anything other than Anais being safe on purpose. This conversation needed to happen in person, and I was willing to wait.

Ellen, my father's long-time assistant, stood up and stared at me, her eyes wide and mouth open. No one stormed into Martin Cross's office and definitely not one of his sons. I wanted to take him by surprise, in hopes that he would do what I wanted him to do: tell the truth. No more hiding behind burying the past and talks of never speaking of this again. He might not have known everything, he knew more than he was letting on, including why Vincent blamed him for his father's death. I wanted answers and I wanted them now.

"Let me see if Mr. Cross is available."

"No need," I said, before brushing past her and knocking on my father's closed office door." Before he could say come in, I waltzed into his office and shut the door behind me.

"To what do I owe this pleasure, Damien? I wasn't expecting you today." Dad placed his pen down and gave me a small smile.

"Can we talk for a minute?"

"Of course, son. I have some time before my next meeting. What do you want to talk about?"

"I want to talk about that night. The night of the fire. I know there's more to the story that you aren't telling me, and I demand to know everything."

Dad's face turned cold. "Why? That's in the past and we buried that."

"No. You buried it and I didn't say anything about it even though I continued to suffer with the aftermath of this for years."

Dad leaned back in his chair with his arms crossed. "Do you want to take a seat before this conversation continues?"

"No. Speaking of things being buried, it seems that things don't stay that way because Charlotte is alive."

Dad sat up with a start, placing his hands on his desk. "Charlotte is what?"

"She's alive. I saw her with my own two eyes." I moved away from the door and walked closer to my father's desk. "There's a lot that you need to be filled in on that I've been keeping quiet while we get things sorted, and it revolves around you and the DePalmas."

"We've both been keeping things from each other, it seems." He said it matter-of-factly.

I agreed, except the secrets that I had been keeping were only a few days old versus his, which were well over a decade. I waited for him to say something else, but he didn't. He almost looked to be in a daze, a reaction I'd never seen on his face.

He snapped out of it and directed his gaze to me. "Charlotte is alive?"

I nodded. "If I hadn't seen her, I wouldn't have believed it either."

"How did you find out?" Dad stood up from his chair and walked toward me. He placed a hand on my shoulder.

"When Anais was kidnapped and met Charlotte while they both were in captivity."

I watched as the information registered. "Is she also okay? Why didn't you call me?"

Why hadn't I? Honestly, I hadn't thought of it. Things were moving so fast with trying to save Anais that it didn't give me an opportunity to tell him while we were on the move. Then I spent most of the last few days making sure that Anais had everything she needed and more.

"Dad, I was taking care of things. That's why I took off or have been working sparse hours from home."

"I thought it was just to take care of Anais, not that all of this other mess was entangled in this. I can't remember the last time when you took off completely. No emails, no meetings from home."

That was accurate. Work didn't matter as much to me right now when the center of my world had been thrown into harm's way.

"We needed to take some time to ourselves as well as get a bunch of things sorted. Charlotte helped save Anais's life, Dad."

I don't know if I've ever seen my father look so shocked.

"That wouldn't be the first time she saved someone's life."

My eyes narrowed as I scanned my father. He looked at the wall to the right of my head before looking back at me. "Care to elaborate?"

Dad looked at me before his eyes glanced at a small table

behind his desk. I knew he was looking at the family photos that he placed there years ago. He sighed and I could see that he was trying to figure out how to approach the situation at hand. I'd seen the same look on his face during many meetings just as he was about to speak. But I spoke first, voicing one of the thoughts that stayed with me all of these years.

"Something I always wondered about that night is who told you that something might occur that made you drive up?"

"I received a phone call on my office line at home. Since it was the weekend, it went straight to voicemail. I ended up checking it about twenty minutes later after dinner with your mother. The voice on the message was soft, but it didn't take much for me to put together that it was Charlotte. She said that you were in danger and that I needed to get up there. I rushed to tell your mother and our house went into lock-down. We decided to send several of our guards to get your brothers, who were at a friend's house, just in case this was a direct attack on our family. I went with my driver to go and get you. We raced up there and I spotted your car when we arrived and made a split-second decision to send my driver back home, because the plan was to drive your car back."

His eyes glazed over once more, as if he was recalling the night in question. I saw a small tear forming in the corner of his eye and when he focused on me, the tear threatened to fall. I could only imagine how he felt when he arrived at the scene, when he didn't know if his first born was alive or dead. It was then that I realized the steadiness that he showcased when we were driving away from the house.

"We saw the smoke coming out of one of the windows on the top floor, but I again told my driver to leave. When he pulled off, I heard a loud bang and that's when I ran toward the house and you know the rest of what happened that night. Son, I had hoped to get her too but, by the way the fire was burning, I—I thought I was already too late. The police said the fire was accidental, but I knew better."

My gut told me something similar, which was why her memory haunted me. But there was one thing that was left unanswered. "How is Harvey involved in all of this?"

This was the first time I had said Will, Vincent, and Charlotte's father's name in years. I had no opinion of him either way because I might have seen him in passing when Dad did business with him, but that was it.

Dad turned away from me and walked back toward his desk. He looked down with his back to me before sitting back down in his office chair. "Harvey was a troubled man. Was involved in things he shouldn't have been in and I bailed him out a few times. When I refused to bail him out again, he had nowhere else to turn. I didn't save him, and he was killed because of it. I assume if Vincent is coming after you, he blames Harvey's death on me."

"And so he took it out on me. I'm sure it didn't help that I was dating his sister."

"I would think so."

"Harvey died just before the fire by his own hand. Why would Vincent wait so long to do anything?"

"If you are now his target, because you escaped the fire, then he waited for you to care about something or someone enough to strike."

I knew my dad was talking about Anais without mentioning her name. "In the end, Charlotte ended up saving not just Anais's life this time, but my life years ago. I don't know if I would have been able to make it out there if she hadn't waited or contacted you. Then if you hadn't gotten there when you did and busted down the front door..."

"Yeah, I guess she did."

"And there is no way I'll ever be able to pay her back... outside of making sure her brother can't do anything to harm any of us again. It's about time we find out what hole Vincent climbed into."

13

ANAIS

"Do you need anything?"

I was in the kitchen preparing sugar cookies and had just placed them in the oven. It was something that I wanted to do to pass the time while I was supposed to be resting. I didn't want to aggravate my recovery and had been trying to find different activities I could do that didn't involve watching a screen.

Thinking about one particular activity brought my attention back to Damien. The question was a loaded one and I stared Damien down. There was something I wanted that Damien seemingly refused to give me. "Yes, there is something I want."

The look on my face must have given my intentions away because Damien slightly shook his head. "No."

"You don't even know what I was thinking."

"Oh, but I do. Because it's the same thing that has been on your mind for the last few days. When I'm going to fuck you next."

One would think that out of all of the things that Damien

and I had done, I wouldn't have a reason to blush anymore, yet his words made my cheeks heat up like an inferno.

"I've never said that—"

"Your eyes betray you, Spitfire. Everything will return to normal in due time."

I knew it would, but that didn't mean that the desire that still burned for him in my body was willing to wait. The time that we had apart when I left our arrangement was nothing compared to this torture. Being around him, yet not touching him intimately was a form of torture.

Damien took a step closer to me and laid a hand on my cheek. Although we lay together in bed at night and his touch brought me comfort and security, it wasn't doing everything I had come accustomed to. I missed when he would showcase how well he knew my body and just how to pleasure it. He tilted my head up and pressed a soft kiss on my lips. There was no heat, no fire.

My hand landed behind his neck and pulled him closer to me, deepening the kiss. I knew he wanted this as much as I did, yet he pulled away. I stared at his lips, wishing they were back on mine.

"I want you to be fully recovered for the activities that I have planned. Only then will we partake in them."

The urge to mock his last sentence was there but I swallowed the retort. The best course of action was to change the subject. "There have been a couple of things that have been on my mind that I've been meaning to ask you."

"Well?"

"This is embarrassing, but when is your birthday?"

"We've never talked about that, have we? July 24."

I sighed. "Now I feel even more like an idiot."

Damien raised an eyebrow at me and stared down into my eyes. "Why?"

"Carter lured me out of here the day he kidnapped me by telling me that there was something happening related to your birthday."

He wiped a piece of my hair away from my face and tucked it behind my ear. "It's not your fault. We spent most of our time together battling versus getting to know the random details about one another. That will change."

His words reassured me, and I knew that he was right. I hoped my next question wouldn't do much damage to the mood that had been created, but it needed to be asked. "Anything new about Vincent?"

Damien's jaw clenched. Clearly that subject was the wrong one. I wondered if he was going to tell me anything else.

"We still don't know where he is. He's all but vanished, but that doesn't mean that I don't have people on the ground who are trying to flush him out. Hopefully, we'll have an update soon."

His answer seemed final, as if he had just closed the door to this conversation. I nodded my head before walking out of the kitchen. Damien followed me into the living room, and I sat down on the black leather couch. I pulled my hair out of its ponytail as Damien followed my lead and sat down next to me. He gently pulled me into his side.

"Do you enjoy living here?"

His question was unexpected. I looked at him for a moment, studying his face as I tried to come up with an answer. "Why wouldn't I?"

"That's not an answer."

I knew it wasn't, but I wanted to take a more measured approach. "I have everything I could ever want here, Damien."

A small smile tugged at his lips. "Is this your way of saying you hate living here much like you hated the engagement ring I gave you?"

My eyes widened slightly before I was able to control myself. I knew he caught my reaction, so I stopped trying to hide it.

"It's not that I don't like living here, it's just not me. Everything that's here besides the clothes that I brought with me or the wardrobe that you bought for me isn't mine. Yes, I'm able to do certain activities that I love here, but nothing here reflects my personality. Plus, I feel so far away from the bustle of New York City." I grabbed Damien's hand and continued, "Once again, it's not that I don't appreciate being able to live in a penthouse, but I associate living here to living in an ivory tower, so far away from the world. I know that this was done to protect me, but I was also kidnapped from here. So, it doesn't really matter where we are. I did like living in your mansion in NoHo as long as I have the ability to make it more me."

"What? Don't you like the black leather couch, the dark furniture, and the big-screen TV on the wall?"

I chuckled. "It's not bad, but there could be a little bit more color in here and in the NoHo mansion, if I'm being honest."

Damien was tossing the idea around in his head. "Well, let's see what we can do about changing things up a bit and what moving back to the mansion would look like. It might not be immediate, but we should be able to make it happen."

I reached over and gave Damien a big hug. When I pulled away, he placed a finger under my chin, lifting my head, and my gaze met his. Without a second thought, he leaned over and kissed me, causing fireworks to shoot off behind my closed eyes. The kiss wasn't as heated as I would have preferred, but nonetheless, it was magical.

When we broke apart. Damien rested his forehead on mine as we slowly caught our breath.

"I think we're getting this compromising thing down pat," I said.

Damien pulled away a tad, but I could still see the sparkle in his eyes. "It's only because I've agreed with most of the things you said. I'm making no promises about things we actually disagree on."

I playfully rolled my eyes. "Well, I'm glad about that."

After a beat, Damien cleared his throat and said, "There's something I've been meaning to tell you."

My stomach dropped for a moment. What could he have been keeping from me? "Go on."

"So, I mentioned that I was acquiring some office space before Carter kidnapped you."

I vaguely remembered him mentioning it, but I nodded my head, encouraging him to continue.

"The deal is looking pretty solid, so I wanted to share it with you."

"That's great news!" I was still somewhat confused about the whole thing because it was rare if ever that Damien went into more detail about one of his acquisitions. "What are you going to move into that office space? Starting another company? Taking over an already established one?"

"As of now, neither of the above."

I raised an eyebrow at him. "Is the building worth that much that it makes sense to buy it outright instead of taking over a company that was already there, move one into the building, or start a new business there?"

"The value of the building didn't matter. I bought it so I can protect the most precious thing in this world to me."

"What's that?"

"You."

I ran what Damien said again through my mind before I responded. "You bought my office building?"

Damien nodded. "I knew there was no way that I would be able to keep you at home or locked up in this 'ivory tower' so I'm doing my best to protect you when you're going to be out and about."

"But Damien, once Vincent is caught—"

"Anais, you will always be in danger because you are associated with me. I have enemies in New York City, hell, probably all over the world waiting for an opportunity to strike without a second thought. It's important to me that I keep you safe and right now the security in your building is atrocious. That's how we think Vincent was able to bring a gun in a box to Jake, who then planted it in your office before Vicki collected your mail?"

Damien had a great point. There was nothing in the form of security that would protect me at the office. "Did you even try to talk to the owners?"

"I did. We were lucky enough and got a screenshot of Vincent dropping the gun off. The owners were hardly cooperative with the investigation and would only give a small amount of information to the police. I took matters into my own hands and made them an offer that they couldn't refuse."

I was floored by what Damien had just said. I knew he would take steps to protect me, but I wasn't prepared for him to spend what had to equal millions, if not billions, of dollars to buy an office building and then retrofit it to be more secure so I would have a safe place to go to work. Not only would he be helping to ensure the security of just me but as a result everyone in that building would have a safer working environment.

"And when the time comes, we can add a daycare in the building. Or hell, one can be added to Cross Tower for that matter."

"What? Why?"

"So, when we have kids, they'll be close by and we won't have to worry about anyone we don't want getting hold of them."

"You want kids?" My eyes went wide. We hadn't spoken about it before and I wasn't sure he wanted them.

"With you, yes."

"I don't know what to say." I stared at him in amazement. "Thank you."

"Those words are all I need outside of you telling me that you love me."

I gave him a small grin. "I love you."

He stepped up to me and pressed his lips upon mine.

14

DAMIEN

"Are you sure this is the place Dave said we should go?"

I looked down the street before I glanced at Broderick and asked, "Do you think I would bring us here if it wasn't?" Broderick shrugged so I continued. "According to Dave's intel, Vincent was here a couple days ago. I don't know if he'll show here again tonight, but it wouldn't hurt for us to scope the place out. Also, it wouldn't hurt to show our faces because you never know who might see us and tell him we were looking for him."

"Good plan, then."

"Sometimes I have those." I smirked at Broderick before turning to knock on a door. We were standing outside of a well-worn door in a shady part of town. I heard what sounded like a scraping noise a second after I knocked. My eyes caught a glimpse of a camera in my peripheral vision. I knew that someone was watching.

A few more seconds passed before the door opened up a

smidge. No one said anything, but it was clear that someone was standing just behind the entrance. It was another moment before the door opened up all the way, creaking on its hinges. The man standing on the other side of the door sized both Broderick and me up before he spoke.

"What business do you have here, Mr. Cross?"

The man standing in front of us definitely got his job in part due to his ability to intimidate based on his stature alone. The gentleman wore a black suit that almost looked too tight for his frame due to his muscles bulging against the fabric, almost daring it to hold on for dear life.

"None. We just came here to have a drink, that's all."

The man continued to look us up and down probably trying to determine whether or not we were lying. After giving it another thought, he moved to the side, allowing us to step through the entryway.

Broderick and I entered a dimly lit hallway. The security guard closed the door and moved around us before he walked down the long and narrow hallway. Broderick and I shared a glance before we followed him. It wasn't long until we reached another door at the end of the hallway. Without a word, the guard opened the door and walked through it. We entered into what looked to be a seedy version of a nightclub.

The moment we stepped through the door all eyes were on us. People were trying to figure out why in the world Damien and Broderick Cross would be at this establishment when we had our own club in the same city. I made sure to make eye contact with several of the patrons, hoping that any of them would tell Vincent that we showed up at his stomping grounds. I knew that word would travel and that someone here more than likely knew what he was up to.

"Well, here you are. Don't start any trouble." If the guard's words hadn't conveyed his message, the tone of his voice accomplished it.

"Wouldn't dream of it." That was only partially true. If I did see Vincent here tonight, there was no telling what would happen. But something told me that wouldn't be the case. I wouldn't be surprised if he received a warning the moment that I stepped foot into the club. I also would make sure he knew that I was looking for him.

Broderick and I strolled over to the bar and found two stools off to the side. Before the bartender noticed us, I glanced over at the selection of liquors and noted that they didn't have some of the more expensive brands that were served at Elevate.

"Can I get you two anything?"

A female bartender was looking over at us as she took care of the water that she was grabbing for someone else.

"Two beers. That one on tap is fine." I looked at Broderick, confirming the drink I selected before turning back to the bartender.

She gave both of us a smile, her gaze lingering on Broderick a little longer than necessary.

That might be useful later.

When she walked away, I turned to Broderick and whispered, "When we are about halfway done with our drinks, I want you to ask her when the last time she saw Vincent was."

"Oh, you saw that she gave me the 'please take me out back and fuck me against the building' eyes too."

I shrugged and gave the bartender a polite smile when she returned. Once again, her eyes stayed on Broderick for a few extra seconds before she went to serve someone else.

Broderick and I would quietly talk to one another as we sipped our beers while I looked around, hoping to catch even a glimpse of Vincent.

"Hey, pretty eyes, have you seen Vincent DePalma around here recently?"

Broderick took the perfect opportunity to question the bartender. We had been sitting here drinking our beers. She had come over once before to ask if we needed anything, but we both declined. When she came over a second time, Broderick pounced.

A light rosy color appeared on her cheeks as she looked back at Broderick before she looked up at the ceiling, trying to recall the last time she saw the person in question. "Um, maybe a couple of days ago? He was in here boasting about how this was his time now and that everyone would finally see what he was all about. He's been talking about how he was going to take everyone who wronged him down for months. Guess whatever thing he had planned was finally happening."

I shared a look with Broderick before I said, "Well, if you see Vincent, tell him that Damien is looking for him. And I'm not the only one."

The bartender's eyes darted from me to Broderick before landing back on me. She nodded her head and went off to check on another customer.

"Am I leaving you here so you can go after her?"

Broderick shrugged. "You mean if you didn't just scare her off? She did provide us with some information. Maybe she deserves a reward."

I snorted. "And I'm sure that you'll be the one to give it to her. Have fun." I stood up and downed the rest of my beer. I tossed a few dollars on the bar and left, my thoughts centering on getting back to Anais as soon as possible.

15

ANAIS

As the days flew by, the physical bruises were fading, but the scars that formed in my mind were still present even as I was trying to get back to my habits and schedule. I was back to working from home and loved being able to contribute to Monroe Media Agency again. Dad was also back at work, which was a relief.

After everything that occurred over the last few weeks, my father's first act when he returned to the office was firing Jake because he had wanted to do it in person instead of having Vicki do it. Last I heard Jake was leaving New York City, which was probably best for all parties involved. Deep down, I knew he was fortunate to leave with his life and if he hadn't helped Damien reach me by giving up the information to the apartment that he had taken photos of me from, he'd probably be dead next to Jon and Carter.

I still hadn't seen or heard from Charlotte. I knew that she had been moved to another undisclosed location, but where? It was definitely for safety since Vincent was still roaming the streets of NYC and was now potentially even more dangerous than when he just had a vendetta against Damien, so I understood the need for secrecy, although I thought having both of us talk with her might help with some of the healing that both Damien and I needed.

While Damien, Kingston, and their men were trying to flush Vincent from wherever he was hiding out, I took a sip of the coffee I had just brewed, needing a small boost to get me through the last ninety minutes of work. I was determined to get through some of my workload after everything that had happened.

I stretched my arms above my head as my phone rang. I picked up the device and glanced at the screen before I answered.

"Hey, Damien."

"Anais."

Listening to the way he said my name would never get old. "Yes, did something happen?"

"No."

I waited for him to elaborate, but he didn't. "Damien, something has to be wrong. You called me instead of texting."

I could hear his low chuckle on the other end of the line, which made me tremble slightly. In his voice, it was easy to tell that he had something up his sleeve. What it was, only he knew.

"I want you to be ready to go in ninety minutes."

I rolled my eyes at his demand. "What are we doing?"

"We're going out on a date."

～

ROB CLOSED the car door after I sat down in the backseat.

"Anything new about Vincent?"

Kingston just shook his head but didn't look up from his phone. It was clear that the Cross men refused to explain anything.

I cleared my throat before I turned my attention to Rob. "How did you and your wife like Colorado? I don't remember if I ever asked with everything going on."

Rob smiled at me in the rear-view mirror. "She loved the time away from the city. I might have gotten a few bumps while skiing, but nothing that I couldn't handle."

"I'm glad you both had a lovely time. I can't remember the last time I'd been on a vacation that was strictly about having fun."

"Where would you go given the choice to go anywhere?"

I thought about it for a moment before I responded. "Probably somewhere almost the complete opposite of where you went. I'd love to spend time on an island, enjoying the sun and getting out of the dreary weather that New York City has had lately."

"That's true, but spring is right around the corner."

Thank goodness. I was over winter as this might have been the worst season of my life. My thoughts ventured toward all that had happened this winter. The biggest standout out of all of it was Damien. I would have categorized him as one of the worst things to ever happen to me. There was no way I could say that now. The journey that we were on together wasn't easy by a long shot. It would be easier to step away and go back to a life that didn't involve Damien at all. But that would be the cowardly approach. I now knew where I needed to be: next to Damien. Seeing how distraught he was after he rescued me and during the early hours of my recovery didn't make me think of him as weak. It took a lot of courage to be vulnerable and I believe that was when our relationship turned a metaphorical page. It made me realize how much he truly cared for me.

"Ms. Monroe? We're here."

I shook away the thoughts that had taken up most of the car ride and looked out the window. We were double-parked outside of a huge building with no signs that gave it away. Thoughts of what happened the last time I went to a restaurant popped into my mind before I was able to swipe them away. I hoped that this evening's adventure wouldn't be a replica of what occurred the last time I had gone out with Damien. Something told me it wouldn't.

Kingston walked with me up to the front doors and I was greeted by a woman in a white button-down shirt and black pants.

"Hello! Welcome to Bella River! How may I assist you?"

"I'm with Damien Cross."

"Ah, yes. Mrs. Cross, right this way."

Kingston stared at the woman with an eyebrow raised before I gave him a small wave. After I had been called Mrs. Cross on the way to see my parents when they were staying in the Hamptons, the slipup didn't seem weird to me and I didn't bother correcting her. The hostess walked inside and once the doors closed, she turned and smiled.

"I know you're going to have a good time here tonight."

"I hope I do too."

"First time here?"

"Yes, it is." I refused to admit that I had never heard of the restaurant before tonight.

"Well, I won't ruin any of the surprises that are in store.

But I do believe that you're going to have a magical experience."

I glanced up from staring at the floor. Her warm smile helped settle some of the nerves I had been feeling since I walked out of the house.

I smoothed the black coat I was wearing down as the elevator came to a stop. When the doors opened, I followed the hostess out and together she and I walked toward another set of doors that looked like it might lead outside.

"After you, Mrs. Cross." She held the door open and let me walk through first.

I found us standing on the roof of the building. I would've expected there to be more people out there, but I couldn't see any from my viewpoint. The sun was starting to set, casting a warm glow, and creating a soft, romantic vibe over the space.

"There you are." The hostess and I turned our heads and found ourselves face-to-face with Damien Cross. "I was wondering when you'd get here."

I turned to the staffer. "Thank you for bringing me up."

"Anytime, Mrs. Cross. Please let me know if either one of you need anything." With that she left us alone, and the beat of silence warmed me briefly even as a light breeze passed between us.

"I don't think I'm late."

"You aren't. I just wished you were able to come sooner."

"Or did you hope that I was late so that you could punish me later?" I took a step toward Damien with a smile.

"That wouldn't have been the worst thing in the world." Damien took a step toward me and closed the gap between us. I noticed that he had unbuttoned the top button of the white button-down he had worn earlier that day. He looked more relaxed than when he had left for work early that morning. He still wasn't back in the office full-time and I loved it. Selfishly, I've gotten Damien to myself. It allowed us to spend more time together with limited interruptions. He leaned down and greeted me with a kiss that I missed deeply. "Good evening to you too."

Damien chuckled. "Do you want something to drink?"

It was then that I realized he had his trademark whiskey in hand. He took a small step back before taking a sip. I nodded because a glass of wine sounded wonderful right now.

"Come this way. The bar is just over here."

I followed Damien's lead as we walked around a corner and I was left speechless. There was a bar with a bartender who gave me a brief smile when I came into his line of sight, but no one else was around. There was a small partially enclosed area where a table was set for two and the only light was the sunset, the candles on the table and the soft string lights that surrounded the bar. There were tons of flowers draped over the enclosed area, creating a sense of springtime, something I so desperately wished it was. A soft melody played in the background, the perfect finisher to what looked to be a masterpiece.

"This is stunning, Damien."

"I'm glad you like it. Come on, let's get you a drink and get us situated so we can start our night." I smiled up at him as he walked over to our table. When I started to slide my coat off my shoulders, I looked down at my dress and said, "This dress isn't appropriate for sitting outside in this weather."

Damien's eyes were staring at the parts of the dress that I had revealed to him when I partially removed the coat. I saw the heat rising in his eyes and my body immediately knew how to react to the attention.

"There are heaters out here but if you get cold, I have no problem asking for us to be moved inside. They should be happy to accommodate."

I took my coat off completely and placed it behind my chair before taking a small step back so he could pull the chair out. He was right and I felt warmer than I thought I would. I had doubts about whether or not this off-the-shoulder, tightly fitted blush dress would be okay for dinner on a rooftop. The dress came up to just above my knee and it had a split that reached midthigh. The tan strappy heels, the gold jewelry, and the tan purse that I chose to wear finished off the outfit. I hoped my more natural makeup brought a soft glow to my face that would be missing this time of year.

"This is all so lovely."

"Thank you. Something told me you would enjoy it because their speciality is seafood cuisine."

I smiled at Damien's attention to detail. I loved seafood and didn't have it as often as I would have liked. The last time I had it was at the fundraiser, just before Jon's murder.

It took no time for us to pick out what we wanted to eat and for me to get served the glass of wine I'd been craving since he mentioned it. We kept the conversation light and breezy, just like the soft wind I felt in this enclosed space. Our dinner was served, and we spent most of that time quietly eating and enjoying the silence that passed between us.

"This lobster tail is taking me on a journey that I didn't know I wanted or needed." I placed the last bit of lobster into my mouth before I wiped my lips. Damien took a sip of his whiskey as I turned my attention to the current melody that was playing over the speakers. "Let's dance."

"I don't dance."

"You don't dance, or you don't want to dance?"

"Both."

I snorted. "You do now, come on, Damien. Humor me. We don't have to do anything fancy, I promise."

Damien hesitated for a moment. Was this the first time I had seen him unsure about something? He pushed his chair back and stood up before he walked over to my side of the table and held his hand out. I stood up as well and allowed him to bring me into his arms as we gently swayed to the soft melody playing on the speakers.

"You know, I debated hiring live music to play here tonight."

"I'm glad you didn't. It might have been a little weird having them sit around and watch us eat and now dance. Tonight's been perfect, just the way it is." Between our slow dancing, his embrace, and his woodsy cologne, I was being lulled into a fantasy where everything was perfect, and danger wasn't lurking behind every corner. It was where Damien and I could just be ourselves with no priorities other than one another.

"I love you."

I still wasn't used to hearing him say those words, yet they warmed my soul and as his lips made their way toward mine, I whispered, "I love you too."

～

"You've been teasing me all night, Spitfire."

I looked around the penthouse before my eyes landed back on Damien. He had just closed the door. "How? I haven't done anything."

"The dress you chose to wear tonight hugs every single curve of your body and I can't wait to strip it off of you. Inch. By. Inch."

Goosebumps appeared on my flesh, giving a glimpse of the effect he was having on my body.

"Turn around."

I did as he said but I wasn't giving in that easy. "Why don't I make things a little easier for you?" I twirled slowly so that my back was to him and reached up, finding the zipper of the dress. I pulled it down, revealing even more skin than before, and looked at him over my shoulder. My heart was pounding with anticipation. The heat that was in his eyes earlier tonight returned with a vengeance and I knew I was in for a wild ride.

Before waiting for him to say another word, I walked out of the room and into the bedroom, adding a little extra sway to my hips as I went. If he was going to accuse me of being a tease, there was no way I wasn't going to live up to it, punishments be damned. By the time I reached the foot of the bed, I heard the bedroom door close with a resounding click.

"Do you think this is a game?"

"No, I—"

"You don't run this. I do." Damien spun me around so that I faced him, pulled me toward him, and kissed me like his life depended on it.

He paused briefly to whip his shirt off before his lips latched on to mine once more. His fingers moved across my back, looking for his end goal, and when he found it, the only noise I could hear was the zipper of my dress moving lower and lower. When the zipper reached its destination, I let the dress fall from my body, leaving me in just a bra and panties.

"Much better."

A drop of self-consciousness appeared before me as he examined my body with only my underwear covering my modesty. Most of my bruises had faded, but I knew I still had a couple that were somewhat noticeable on my skin. I let out a deep breath and cleared the worry from my mind. These were some temporary scars on my body because I survived something traumatic. And if the way Damien was looking at me was any indication, he couldn't care less.

Without breaking eye contact, he reached behind me and unsnapped my bra and it fell to the floor. "Lie down on the bed."

Without looking behind me, I sat down on the bed and before I had a chance to suck in a breath, he was on me. His lips tasted my neck before making their way to my breasts. He took his time massaging my breasts and sucking on my nipples. He alternated between which breast would get attention, so I didn't know what was coming next. He licked my left nipple once more before he looked at me and stood up.

He took a second to step back and toss a condom on the bed that he pulled out of his pocket. While he undid his pants, I took a moment to admire his bare chest, which was crafted to perfection from his neck down to his six-pack.

Damien moved back over me, his fingers going farther south. When he reached the apex of my thighs, he shifted the flimsy fabric of my thong out of the way and replaced it with his fingers. "Oh fuck, you're so wet for me."

He slowly removed my panties and I almost growled. "If

you don't stick your cock in me and fuck me within the next five seconds, I'll—"

"You'll do what, Spitfire?"

He didn't give me an opportunity to answer because I felt the head of his dick at my entrance. The anticipation was going to kill me, I was sure of it. When he finally sunk his cock into me, I sighed with relief. I'd missed this connection with him so much.

"Damien, I'm not fragile like expensive china. When I said I wanted you to fuck me, I meant it."

"Whatever the lady wants, the lady gets."

When he pushed all the way into me, my eyes closed as I took a moment to enjoy the sensations of having him inside my pussy. He picked up the tempo and I moaned as his cock was hitting all of the places that I needed him to hit. His pace continued to quicken and soon he was fucking me the way I wanted to be fucked.

"Yes, oh my..." I couldn't find the words to express how good this felt. My eyes fluttered shut. "I'm close."

"You can only come when I say so."

"What?" My eyes sprung open and landed on Damien.

"You can't come until I say so. That's payback for your little striptease earlier."

"You've got to be fucking kidding me."

"No. I'm fucking you, but I'm not kidding. Take all of this, Spitfire."

I should have known he would find a way to punish me for the stunt I pulled earlier, but I didn't know it would be right now. I focused on not orgasming as Damien moved in and out of me, his smirk telling me that he was enjoying this too much. I groaned and closed my eyes tightly as I tried to prevent what had become my body's natural instinct. This was unbearable.

"Come, Anais."

"Yes!" The word came out as a hiss as I was finally able to orgasm.

Relief and ecstasy flooded my body as I finally gave in to what my body was seeking. Damien groaned as he found his own release. He lay down on top of me and the only thing that could be heard between the two of us was our panting as we tried to catch our breaths.

"We can never go that long without sex," I said.

"You read my mind. Deal."

16

DAMIEN

"Is Charlotte going to be here? She might know something that might help."

"Will didn't say whether or not she would be."

"I hope so. She helped save my life and I want to, at the very least, thank her for that."

"Makes sense to me."

"Thanks for letting me come with you. I know you usually handle business like this on your own."

"Yes, I usually do. But I wanted to give you another peek inside of my world. Is that alright?" I said slowly. This was another way I was trying to fix things. This situation involved her directly and she should be in the room to give her opinion and make decisions.

Anais hesitated before she said, "Okay." I could see the skepticism in her eyes. She would soon learn how serious I was about making things right. I held open the wooden brown door and allowed Anais to walk in first. A woman sitting at a reception desk looked up at us.

"Can I help you?"

"Yes, can you tell your boss that Damien Cross and Anais Monroe are here to see him?"

"Ah. They are expecting you, just give me one moment."

The woman picked up the phone and announced our presence to the person on the other end. When she hung up, she gave us a tight smile before she spoke.

"I'll show you to the conference room."

She walked around the desk and opened a door. She walked through first and held it open for us before she started walking down a short hallway with us following behind her. The receptionist approached another brown door and gently knocked before opening it and gesturing for us to go in. I nodded my head in acknowledgment and Anais whispered a quick thank-you before we entered.

"Damien, Anais. Welcome to my office." Will stood up from the table and stuck out his hand to shake.

I returned the gesture and as he moved to shake Anais's hand, my eyes landed on the woman who seemed to be a blessing and a curse to my life. Charlotte stood up and shook my hand too and I noticed the air in the room had changed from indifference to awkwardness. Given what this conversation was going to be about, I wasn't surprised. Anais moved around me and hesitated as she stared at Charlotte, before she said, "Is it okay if we hug?"

A smile appeared on Charlotte's face. "Of course."

The two women embraced, and Will and I gave them their moment as we picked seats at the long table. Yes, Charlotte and I had a history, but they deserved to take as much time as they needed given what they had both been through. Together.

When the women broke apart, Anais said, "I owe you so much."

I stood up to walk over to Anais when her voice broke, but she looked over at me and mouthed that she was okay.

"No, you don't. We both worked together to escape, and it worked."

"It doesn't make anything you did less heroic."

"It goes both ways, Anais."

The women hugged again before taking their seats. I pulled out my handkerchief and gave it to Anais, who used it to do dab at the corners of her eyes.

Will spoke up this time. "Let's cut straight to the chase, shall we?" He leaned back in his chair, his eyes coolly assessing the situation.

"I agree."

"How are you doing, Anais?"

I lightly cleared my throat, daring him to say something else. Anais placed her hand on my knee, and I could read the warning in her eyes. "She's not what this discussion is about."

I knew many people didn't threaten Will, but I couldn't care less. I was just as dangerous as he was, if not even more so. He couldn't run his operations without me, so it was best if he stayed on my good side.

"I can speak for myself, Damien. I'm fine, Will. Thanks for asking. How are you, Charlotte?"

"Better."

"Do you have any updates on Vincent?"

Will shook his head. "He knows he's a dead man when I find him."

Of course, Will didn't know his location. That would

make things too easy. "You don't have anyone tracking him? He can't be this hard to find."

"Well, have you found him yet?"

He did have a point. "No, but he wasn't doing legwork for any of my businesses either."

Will rubbed a hand across his chin. "Vincent hasn't worked for the Vitale family ih years. He disappeared years ago and to be honest, I fully expected to get a call at some point that his body had been found. With everything going on now, I've had my men trying to find him and we've been able to find a trail of breadcrumbs that has painted somewhat of a picture of what he's been doing over the years. Apparently, he's been building relationships with other organizations in the city, doing odds and ends for them in exchange for favors and their silence about his whereabouts. Explains the capital he was able to gather in order to do everything he's done so far. He doesn't hang around his usual haunts and hasn't been answering calls from anyone. The only people he might be willing to try to find are you or Charlotte at this point."

That thought crossed my mind. If he had gone as far as to hire someone to kidnap his sister after she spent years in hiding and came after what was mine, he had to have been planning this for a while. But what was his ultimate goal? Did he still want to get back at me? Kill Charlotte for disobeying him years ago? I had no doubt that he was planning something to strike back. It was just a question of what and when. And how could we get him before someone else got hurt?

I set those thoughts aside for the time being because we had some other issues that needed to be resolved.

"Charlotte, you and I have some things to discuss."

She nodded. "I know. What can I answer for you?"

"Although I assume I know the answer, I still want to hear it from you. Why did you pretend to be dead for all of these years? Were you hiding from Vincent?"

Charlotte looked at her brother before she looked down at her hands. "What was the thing I told you before the fire?"

An image of Charlotte at eighteen flashed through my mind. We had sat down on the couch in our home for the weekend about to tear into some pizza when she stopped from eating. "You told me that I needed to be careful, and I asked you why and you said you just had a bad feeling."

"That's because I knew Vincent was going to do something that weekend. I knew because he recruited me to bring you up there to burn you alive."

I tightly gripped the arms of the chair that I was sitting in to avoid jumping out of my seat. "He did what?"

Charlotte sighed. "Vincent was convinced that your father led my father to kill himself. I overheard Vincent talking to someone on the phone about the situation shortly after we started dating. The gist I got from it was that my father owed Martin a lot of money because he lost some of the merchandise Martin was supposed to buy from him. Martin wasn't willing to forgive the debt and that caused my father to spiral until he ended it all. Vincent caught me, called me into his office, and it was like a light bulb went off in his head and he concocted this plan that I was supposed to help him carry out in order to get revenge for our father's death. Vincent told me I was as good as dead to him if I didn't help, and how dare I ruin Dad's legacy."

Charlotte took a moment and looked over at Will again, who nodded. "So I did it, I invited you up for the weekend and immediately regretted it. I debated going to the police but knew that if Vincent knew it was me who ratted, he would have me killed. I wanted to warn you that Vincent was acting deranged and wanted you dead, but I worried about what the end result of that would be for me too. A few hours before the house was supposed to go up in flames, I called your father and told him to come and get you and when you went downstairs for a drink of water, I signaled to Vincent before I climbed out of the window and I ran. I prayed that your father got to you in time and I just ran. It was cowardly I know, but—"

"But what choice did you have? We were still in high school and you did your best to warn someone who could do something about it. You saved my life as well."

Tears formed in Charlotte's eyes. "You wouldn't have been up there if it weren't for me."

"You ended up saving both of our lives, although I'm sure yours changed dramatically when you ran."

Charlotte nodded. "I debated calling Will, but I didn't want to drag him into all of this either, so I took off and never looked back."

This was the first time I felt at peace with what happened that night. Charlotte's explanation made sense and I could easily tell that she was caught between two terrible outcomes and had done her best to forge her own path ahead. Her efforts worked until Vincent started causing trouble years later.

"Thanks for giving an explanation, Charlotte."

She gave me a small smile before I turned to Will. "We'll head out, but if you find anything, you'll contact me."

I saw the smirk appear on Will's face before he could remove it. "Is that an order?"

"Your words, not mine. I'll be in touch." I stood up from the chair and walked toward the guard standing by the door.

"Damien."

I paused and turned to look over my shoulder at the man sitting behind the great big desk that almost reminded me of my father's at my childhood home.

"If you find Vincent before I do, I want him back. Dead or alive."

"Deal."

"I FEEL like we're getting closer to Vincent, yet we still have a ways to go. Turns out he went rogue, and Will doesn't know where he is either. I think he got the message about what happened to Carter loud and clear and ran. Will is looking for him too." My leg bounced up and down at my desk while I chatted on the phone hours after the meeting with Will and Charlotte after Anais went to bed. She was drained from the meeting earlier today.

"I'm not surprised. We're digging through some of the devices we found at Carter's apartment and the cabin to see if that would give us any leads. We are also digging into both of their backgrounds to see if anything pops."

"Are you working with Dave?" I mentioned the name of the person we usually called on to find everything there was to find about someone.

"Yes. Uncle Martin authorized it."

"You didn't tell me you spoke to my father."

"Must have slipped my mind. He knows everything now. Might be helpful to dig up any known associates of Harvey as well. They might be helping Vincent now."

That might be helpful. Anything that could get us closer to him would be key. I knew that if Will found him before I did, I wouldn't get a chance at him. I would be happy to deliver his body to them once I was finished with him, so we had to find him first.

"Did they have anything to say about us finding him? I'm not keeping it quiet that I'm hunting him down."

"No one is stepping on anyone's toes here. Will understands why you'd be going after him. He fucked with what was yours and he doesn't care as long as the end result is the same."

"Let me know if you hear anything else."

"You got it."

I hung up the phone and stared at my computer screen. *Where do we go from here?*

Thoughts of how to lure Vincent out circled in my mind but I kept coming back to the only thing that seemed like a sure deal: when he was going to strike again.

17

DAMIEN

I finished typing an email to Melissa when my phone buzzed on my desk. Who would be calling at this time of night?

I had slipped out of bed while Anais slept in hopes of getting some work that might make me tired enough to fall asleep beside her. I looked over at the caller ID and closed my eyes. Why was he calling me when we had already met earlier today? I took a deep breath and answered the phone. "Damien."

"He killed a couple of my men. I thought he might attack because he probably thought I was involved due to Charlotte."

"Son of a bitch." I ran a hand through my hair, making even more messy than it was before. I made a note to check in with Dad after this just in case Vincent tried to go after him because it seemed as if his target on me was shifting. "How did it happen, Will?"

"He, or someone he must be working with, snuck and

attacked them while they were out on a run for me. This fucker has to pay and I'm growing impatient."

"I know. Any word on his whereabouts?"

"No. You know I would've reached out to you if I heard anything."

"Would you have though? I think you wouldn't have hesitated to kill me over Jon's disappearance just a week ago, even though he was an asshole. You'd have taken me out without even a blink of the eye."

"Touché," Will said before taking a deep breath. "There has to be more we can do to get to him. I don't know how long I can patiently wait for something in this case before we find him. Brother or not, I will not allow for there to be more fucking blood spilled unless it's his. This needs to end."

I rubbed my hands across my face, mentally going through the information that has been gathered. What were we all missing? This man couldn't have that many resources to be able to hide for this length of time. "I've already stepped things up a notch by going to his old stomping grounds and I've talked with some people I know have done business with him. In other words, he has to know I'm looking for him. Let's give it a few days to see if my inquiring pisses him off enough and causes him to resurface."

"Okay and I'll see what I can do on my end."

THE NEXT MORNING, I couldn't help but smile. Anais had no idea what was coming. It was time for us to do something for her and that was a promise that I took seriously.

My urge to get her out from the city was intense due to

Vincent still being on the run. I decided to take her away for a bit while I waited to see if Vincent would appear. Since I didn't know how long it would take, secretly getting away for a bit would be fun and rejuvenating, something I thought Anais desperately needed. When we returned, it would be time to enact a new plan if mine didn't work. I was determined that everyone in this situation wouldn't live in fear any longer, particularly Anais and Charlotte.

Now it was time to take Anais's mind off this. I made a few arrangements myself and had Melissa finish up the rest. I tossed a card in front of Anais while she was sitting on the couch.

"What's this?" she asked as she looked down at the white cardstock and flipped it around in her hands.

"I didn't know you had trouble reading."

I watched as she rolled her eyes, making a note to myself that she would pay for that later. She finally read the card and then it slipped from her hands and fell to the floor.

"We're going to St. Barts?"

"Oh, so you do know how to read," I said, folding my arms over my chest. I tried to contain my happiness over her being excited, but I couldn't. This was the happiest she had been in weeks and it was me that put that smile on her face.

"When do we leave?"

"Tomorrow morning."

She sat forward and the shock was still evident on her face. If she stayed like that long enough, I would have no issue putting my cock in her mouth.

Anais hopped off the couch and into my arms. I was somewhat worried, about what that movement might hurt her head, but she seemed fine as her bright smile flashing back at me.

"How did you know? Did Rob tell you?"

"I don't divulge my secrets."

Anais laughed. "I don't know how I could thank you for this. There is nothing I would be able to do that would ever compare."

"Don't think that way...but there are several ways I can think of you might be able to make it up to me."

ONCE WE WERE SETTLED and up in the air, Anais turned to me and said, "You know one thing I've never done?"

"Gone to St. Barts?"

"Besides that."

"What?"

"Joined the mile-high club."

I raised an eyebrow at her. "Is this your way of dropping a hint?"

"I'm glad you got it. Plus, I already know you have a bed and everything in the back of this jet. This is practically a hotel with wings."

I nodded, agreeing with her assessment. She turned back around and smiled at me. I couldn't help myself and tucked a piece of hair behind her ear and laid a kiss on her lips.

"Get up. We're going to start the initiation process and I can't wait to have your pussy in my face. I want you to go to the bedroom and remove all your clothes. You'll have less than a minute."

Anais glanced toward the front of the plane, probably

looking to see if the flight attendant was nearby. She unbuckled her seat belt and quickly walked toward the back room. I counted to twenty slowly before I joined her.

"Lean over the bed."

Watching her stand there with her ass up in the air teased me and made my cock twitch as I thought of all the things that I could do to her from that position.

"I thought you wanted to eat my pussy?"

"There are a lot of things I want to do to you, but I've decided to get to the pussy eating later. I want to worship this ass for now." I removed my clothes and tossed a condom on the bed. I watched her for a moment then moved closer to her and ran a finger up and down her slit. "Fuck...you're dripping already."

"Tell me something I don't know."

I slapped her ass after her sarcastic comment. It didn't have its intended effect because she was still smirking at me. So, I slapped her ass again, this time choosing the other butt cheek. A moan left her lips, encouraging me to take things up a notch.

"You're enjoying this, aren't you?" I finished my question with another slap on that ass that soon turned into another slap. "I haven't done my due diligence in appreciating this masterpiece."

I laid soft kisses on her back as I gently massaged the flesh I just tormented. When I made my way back down to her cunt, a low groan flew out of my mouth. "You're even wetter than before."

"I want your cock inside me."

"Is that right?" My cock grew harder at her words, begging to be inside of her pussy immediately.

She eagerly nodded her head and when she looked at me over her shoulder, it wasn't hard to tell that she was already halfway there. As I removed the condom wrapper, Anais shook her head.

"What's wrong?"

"Forget the condom. I've been on birth control this entire time."

I raised an eyebrow. "That would have been something to tell me months ago."

"You didn't ask and we don't need it. I'm clean."

"As am I." I flipped her over, lining up our bodies. I teased her entrance with my cock for a few seconds before I guided myself into her cunt. The sensations that I felt without the condom were like night and day and I wondered why we hadn't done it sooner.

Anais shivered when I was fully seated in her. I leaned down to kiss her square on the lips before I started moving my hips. The sounds that left her were like music to my ears and I picked up the pace.

"Yes!" she said, and I could see her losing control.

The wanton-look in her eyes shone through just before her eyes closed. I felt my own release building as I reached down to play with her nipples. We continued at this rapid pace, both of us enjoying one another and seeking salvation on the other end. When I felt her pussy tighten around my cock, I knew her release was imminent. With one final scream, she arched her back and we both let go. Heavy breathing was the only thing that surrounded us as we stared into each other's eyes.

When our breathing slowed down, I said, "Welcome to the mile-high club. I hope you enjoy your stay."

18

ANAIS

I sat in the car and watched in awe as we passed some of the sites that St. Barts had to offer on the way to where we would be staying. I couldn't believe I was here. I couldn't remove the smile from my face as our personal chauffeur took us to our home away from home. I couldn't wait to frolic around in the water at one of the beaches on the island. When I took my eyes off what was going on outside of my window for a moment, they landed on Damien, who was staring at me.

"What? Is there something on my face?"

"No. I'm just watching you."

"That's not creepy at all," I said with a smile before turning my attention back to the window. I was shocked that we were in St. Barts on our first official vacation with one another. Hell, I never thought we would have ever gone anywhere after our deal was up because I didn't want to. Yet here we were, about to enjoy a few days in the Caribbean sun.

"I'm surprised you didn't take me to a private island that you owned or something."

"That's for the next trip."

"Did you just tell a joke? I can't believe it."

Damien shook his head at me before looking back down at his phone, I assume checking in on some of the things that were going on at his office. The view in front of me was already one of the most beautiful things I had ever seen, and it was all flying past me too fast for me to appreciate it. I hoped that the place where we would be staying had a stunning view that I could just stare at for hours if I wanted to.

I smiled. Who was I kidding? Damien Cross always booked the best of the best. And that's just what I saw as we were coming up to the grounds that I assumed we would be staying at for the next few days. There was enough space to fit at least twelve people given the number of bedrooms. That worked out well for us because we had a couple of guards who traveled with us and would be staying here. The private chauffeur, chef, and butler were an added bonus to go along with the private access to the beach. I was dying to try the spa that was located in the basement. Plus getting back into the spirit of working out regularly wouldn't be a bad idea and the fully equipped gym provided enough incentive.

Our security detail came downstairs and chatted with us briefly about securing the villa. When I saw our butler for our stay bringing in the last of our bags, I excused myself and walked over to him.

"Thank you so much for helping us bring our stuff inside."

"It was a pleasure."

Damien appeared by my side and placed an arm around my waist. "We can handle the bags from here."

I turned and found Damien looking at me just as the gentleman turned to leave us to ourselves.

"What?" I looked back at the retreating man before turning to Damien. "I was just thanking him for helping us with our stuff."

"That's unnecessary."

"Green is not your best color."

It took him a second to understand what I meant. "I'm hardly jealous. I was just letting him know that his services were no longer needed."

"You know, you didn't show much of your jealous side when we were back in New York. Well outside of that moment just before we traveled to the Hamptons."

"Things happen. Times change. Speaking of change, we should get changed."

He was right. The clothes we had on were for colder weather in New York.

"Well, if you don't mind bringing our bags up now that you declined the help, I can find something to change into." With that, I spun on my heel and turned to pick out which bedroom we would be staying in on the upper level. I knew I would pay for my little stunt later and I was looking forward to it.

The villa was decorated in bright yet soothing colors creating a relaxing vibe. It was easy to see that the décor was inspired by the country we were in. I was already mentally making plans to return, and I hadn't even been here for half a day yet. I heard some noises behind me and turned to see Damien bringing in my bags.

"Thank you." I walked over and brought his face down to me and laid a sensual kiss on his lips.

"For?"

"Bringing me here and for bringing up my bags."

He smiled briefly before walking toward the doorway. "Do you want anything to eat?"

"I would love a little something. The other thing I would like is some company while I take a shower. You know if you're not too busy conquering another company."

Damien looked at me with a dark gleam in his eye. "It just so happens that my schedule is completely free for the next few days other than fucking you. Get in the bathroom, Spitfire."

"Do we ever have to go back?" I asked, floating along in the infinity pools at the villa Damien rented out. The two guards that were here with us were seated on a couple of lounge chairs nearby but were doing anything but relaxing. I could see them scanning the perimeter every chance they got. With Vincent still at large, Damien thought it was better to be safe than sorry, although even he doubted Vincent would do anything in St. Barts. Damien thought that if Vincent would want to put on a show, and he'd do it in New York City to showcase his power and get the most media attention. Who knew if he would actually admit to the crime but he would revel in media attention surrounding it. Avenging his father's death would be all that he would need.

"We do but not for a little while."

"Well, I'm enjoying this very much. Excellent thoughts and planning on your part." I could see some crinkling at the corners of his eyes, which let me know that he had enjoyed that compliment. The sun was shining brightly, and we were lying under a deep blue sky. It was a picture-perfect moment. And I swore I had only seen such vivid beauty in paintings.

The sound of Damien's phone ringing brought us both out of the moment of bliss that we were feeling. He swam over to the edge of the pool and pulled himself out. He grabbed a towel to wipe himself off before he picked up his phone.

"Kingston sent a text." He walked over to the pool and placed the phone just out of reach.

"I'm going to call him back and put it on speaker phone so we can all hear what he needs to say."

"And I'm going to stay right here, basking in the sun in paradise no matter what he says."

He shook his head and called Kingston back.

"I hope I didn't interrupt anything."

I thought about telling him that he had interrupted some quiet time that I was enjoying spending with Damien, but I didn't.

"Don't worry about it. Anais and your team members are here too. What's up with the 'call me asap' text?"

Kingston got straight to the point. "Vincent has resurfaced. Dave has been helping us tail him."

"What do we have on him? Do we know where he is? Do you think it's time to bring someone in to take him out?"

"Yeah, he crossed into our territory and tried to get into Elevate last night. We confirmed it this morning and I called you immediately."

"Are you serious? By the way, hi, Kingston," I chimed in from my spot in the pool.

"Hello. Yes, it confirms that he is still in the city and

maybe he thought you might be there? Who knows? It also shows that he doesn't give a fuck about anything if he thought he was going to get into Elevate and do whatever he had planned."

"Without a doubt."

"Do you want me to step up security at all of your properties in the city and send a couple more folks to St. Barts?"

I watched as Damien thought about Kingston's proposal. "To me it makes sense, at least for now. If he's brazen enough to come to Elevate, which is heavily guarded, who knows what else he is trying to pull?"

Damien nodded. "Anais is right. We'll step up security and then evaluate once we are back in the city."

"Sounds good," Kingston said.

"The plan is working. I should have an update for you within the hour. Hell, it might have been the reason Vincent resurfaced to begin with."

I raised an eyebrow at Damien. What was he talking about and why was he being purposely vague about it?

"Okay. Thanks for the update. If anything else comes up, let me know." Damien turned to look at me. "I'd do anything to keep her safe."

"I know that. We've all seen how much she has changed you. For the better, I might add."

"I'll talk to you soon."

"Have a good one."

Damien hung up the phone and tossed it on one of the lounge chairs.

"Well, that's a way to bring the mood down. What plan are you doing?"

Damon looked at me before looking out at the pool.

"Kingston and I, along with his team, are working together to find a way to lure Vincent out of hiding and this might be showing that our efforts are working. Anyway, enough about this. Do you want one of those fruity drinks you are in love with?"

"Yes, a piña colada would be great." Why did I get the feeling that there was something he wasn't telling me?

19

ANAIS

I sighed and leaned my head back on the edge of the bathtub, allowing the warm jets to soothe my aching muscles. This included the tenderness between my thighs after Damien gave me his all just a couple of short hours ago as a gentle reminder of what he could do to me. I made a note to myself to get some sort of spa session in before I left the island.

Ellie's words about not becoming addicted to him floated to the surface. I knew I was long past that, however. He had ruined me for any other men who might come along in the future and I could say without hesitation I didn't want anyone else.

But I still felt as if a ticking time bomb was waiting to go off with the potential to take everything that I had worked so hard to build down with it.

What was I thinking, falling in love with Damien Cross? Although he was still demanding, I could easily see that things were getting better. He listened to me more and tried to understand my opinions about certain things. Although at times, he would still say a comment that came across as a demand and that was supposed to be the be-all and end-all. When he did that and I didn't agree, a debate would ensue, and I was perfectly happy with that.

I thought back to some of the fun that we'd had in St. Barts whether it was lounging on the beach, visiting some of the local sites, or getting Damien to try new fruity drinks. Damien rented a catamaran to take us to a small private island where we enjoyed snorkeling, an activity I'd never done before. We got to enjoy swimming with the sea turtles and other tropical fish, and it quickly became one of the best memories I'd ever had. The scrumptious breakfast and lunch that we had catered by a private chef capped off a beautiful day.

I also couldn't forget about the sexcapades we were getting into while on the island as well. We'd taken our time exploring every inch of our bodies over multiple surfaces in this villa and I enjoyed every minute of it. I knew Damien knew how to make my body sing but being in paradise was an additional aphrodisiac.

I glanced down at myself, happy with the glowing, tanner skin I was sporting due to my time in the sun. When the water started to cool down, I stood up and took my time stepping out of the tub and drying myself off. I took even more time moisturizing and throwing a robe over my naked body before I opened the door to leave the bathroom.

It was there that I was greeted with several bouquets of red tulips and roses sitting on the dresser in the bedroom. I knew for a fact they weren't there when I got into the tub and a quick look around confirmed that I was alone. Where had Damien gone? I picked them up and smelled them. They were beautiful and their color reminded me of the red roofs we saw in Gustavia when we went exploring yesterday.

I smelled the flowers once more before putting them back and turned around to find another surprise for me on the bed. A long silky cream-colored dress was lying on the bed next to a white square note.

Put this on and come into the living room.

"Damien, what are you up to?" I muttered to myself before I put the dress on. It reminded me of the silky navy dress that I had worn when I met Jon for the first time at that business dinner. I put on some light makeup and took my hair out of the braid I had placed it in after I washed my hair and before I soaked in the spa tub letting the soft dark waves kiss my shoulders. I walked out into the living room and smiled when I saw Damien sitting on the edge of the couch.

"Hey," I said softly.

He looked up at me with an unreadable expression on his face. He didn't say anything as he stood up and walked over to me. He held his hand out and I placed my hand in his as he guided me to the stairs.

"What's going on?"

"Watch your step."

Flower petals were laid on the floor, creating a path leading to the main floor of the villa.

Nerves bubbled under the surface when he still didn't elaborate. "Damien, what is all of this?"

"Me making up for lost time."

"Wait, what are—"

I was speechless. The main floor had been completely transformed since I had gone upstairs to shower and then soak in the tub. The overhead lights were low, and the living area was lit up by candles with flower petals on the floor and sparsely spread out on the dining room table. Light music played in the background and the glass door was open into the backyard, allowing for a soft breeze to enter, turning into a complete romantic oasis. The furniture had been rearranged to make the room look more open concept.

"What's wrong?"

"Nothing. Everything is perfect."

A sweet smile appeared for a brief second on his face. "Good. I thought we deserved to have a date night while in paradise. I thought about pulling something together on the beach, but you were complaining about the sand and—"

I couldn't stop the grin that wanted to burst out immediately. "No, I wasn't!"

Damien gave me a knowing smirk before he led me over to the dining room table. "Hungry? I thought something lighter might be appropriate because you mentioned you weren't hungry before going upstairs."

The staff at the resort had put together an enormous feast for two people. Instead of having one big meal, there were a lot of appetizers, but enough of them to make up a full meal. If this was what Damien called light...

I grabbed as much food as I wanted and walked over to the couch as I waited for Damien. He soon joined me with food in hand before he left again to get our drinks. Once he was back, we chatted and ate the food in front of us, just like any regular couple would.

Damien cleared his throat and turned to me. "This would be of interest to you. Cross Industries is thinking of starting a new social media network."

My head nearly spun off my neck at his comment. "You're

what? How come you've never mentioned it before? That's incredible!"

"It was a work in progress for a while and I wanted to wait until we had a mock-up before sharing the news."

"Mock-up, huh? Well, grab it, please! I can't wait to see it."

"I'll pull it up on the big screen here. I'm sure some of the images will be familiar to you."

That was when I saw that he brought his laptop down and had it already hooked up to the television. *He is really prepared for anything.* I crossed my legs as the presentation started and was amazed by the sight before me. The crisp colors, the layout of the website, and so much more were pulled together nicely.

I looked over at him and asked, "When is this going to go live?"

"Maybe in the next year or so. Keep watching."

I flipped my eyes back over to the screen and saw that in order to show the website's layout, a fake profile was made featuring photos of me and some of us. Some I recognized from events that we attended, but others I hadn't realized that Damien even took. I glanced at him again when he came over and sat down next to me and smiled as he took my hand into his.

"Our relationship started off rocky to say the least, and I've thought about how much of a selfish prick I was when it came to you." His words made me swallow hard. "Anais, there are so many reasons why you should have run as fast as you could away from me. There are so many reasons why I should have let you go time and time again. You deserve to live a happy and wonderful life and I debated whether or not I can be the one that can give it to you."

"Damien, I agree and it's taking me some time to realize where I want to be and that's with you. This isn't because you're holding a contract over my head or anything like that. I appreciate what we've grown into no matter how we began."

"We've been through a lot together in the short time that we've known each other, and I'm determined to show you how much I love you and wash away any thoughts that you have that this engagement isn't real. I'm doing things differently this time. Marry me."

I chuckled. "When most people propose to someone else, they ask the person versus make a demand."

"That's not my style but I can try it out right now. Anais, will you marry me?" Damien held out a small black box and opened it.

"Oh my—" Any other words died on my lips because the ring in front of me left me stunned beyond belief. "When did you get this? Did you ever find out what happened to the other ring?"

Damien shook his head. "Forget the other ring. I heard this was more along the lines of what you wanted."

All I could do was nod as I stared at the beautiful piece of jewelry in front of me. The ring was much smaller than the one he originally gave me and instead of a huge diamond on the band, he'd replaced it with an emerald. Tears formed in my eyes as they darted between staring at the ring and the man in front of me.

"Yes, yes, I will marry you!" The tears were soon a victim of gravity and there was nothing that could stop their downward trajectory. This was the story I couldn't wait to tell our children ten years down the line. This was the moment I craved with the man I desired more than anyone before.

Damien placed the beautiful ring on my finger, and I took a moment to stare at it before I found myself staring into his beautiful blue eyes. He softly wiped each tear that was falling from my face before he pulled me in for a mind-altering kiss.

His lips moved toward my neck before he said, "Bedroom now."

There was the Neanderthal coming out to play. I grinned when an idea popped into my head. I quickly stood up and took off running toward the stairs. I grabbed the fabric of my dress, pulling it up so I didn't trip.

Damien didn't follow behind me immediately, so I ran past the bedroom we were sleeping in to another one that was unoccupied.

Damien didn't leave me alone for long. "Spitfire, I'm going to fuck you wherever I find you."

My heart thundered in my chest, excitement building as I heard him enter the bedroom next to where I was. I slid farther into the room, hoping to hide from him just a little bit longer. That only bought me several seconds. Soon he was in the doorway, stalking toward me.

"There you are." Damien had already removed his clothes and was holding his dick. *Always prepared.*

"Here I am."

He took another step toward me and I took a step back. The pattern continued and my pulse quickened with each move we made. In the dull light, his feelings were flashing in his eyes like neon lights. He was ready to claim me as his once more. I felt my back hit the wall. There was nowhere else to go, nowhere else to hide.

Damien ran a finger along the thin straps holding my dress on me. "This will have to go. Lift your arms."

"But—" I looked out the window before looking back at him, knowing there might be a chance that we could be seen.

"The only person you need to worry about seeing you naked tonight is me."

That was when he pulled the silky dress over my head, leaving me completely bare to him. His eyes perused my body before he started his attack on me again. Every lick and nibble was meant to drive me wild.

My gaze didn't waver once they met his again as I did as he asked, and the dress was tossed to the side like yesterday's trash. He took both of my hands in one of his and held them against the wall. Still, I kept my eyes on him, refusing to be intimidated.

"You didn't put anything on underneath the dress. Excellent." One hand held my hands on the wall as the other moved down my body to my pussy. "That chase made you wet for me, didn't it?"

"Maybe." I let the word lazily roll off my tongue.

"Are you ready? We can take it slower later."

"Yes, please." My voice came out in a breathless whisper.

"Your arms will stay up in that position until I tell you when you can move them."

I nod quickly, hoping that would get Damien to move faster toward our goal. Damien slowly moved his hand from my pussy and toward my calf and lifted my leg around his waist. He did the same with my other leg and I growled in frustration.

"Getting impatient, Spitfire?"

I almost didn't hear his question due to him moving my body so that my pussy lined up with his cock. Without a second thought, Damien entered me completely and I moaned because he didn't stop until he was completely inside of me.

"Fuck, how is it that I already want you again and we haven't fucked yet?"

"Our bodies are addicted to one another, that's why." My words stopped abruptly due to him slamming into me again. And again. And again. The wall was allowing Damien to fuck me from a different angle, and it felt glorious. The only thing that could be heard between us was our heavy breathing and our bodies becoming one.

I could feel the sweat gathering on my back as Damien pounded into me.

"Do you want to come?" Damien's words came out as more of a series of grunts, but I understood him just the same.

"Yes, oh God, yes!" I said and felt my body begin to shake against his. As I rode the wave of my orgasm, he continued thrusting into me.

"Anais..." Damien groaned as he too found his release. Both of us stared at each other without making any moves to break our connection anytime soon.

"Is Cross Industries really creating another social media platform?"

Damien chuckled. "There have been talks, but I don't have any concrete information. What I do have is another smaller surprise for you."

I lifted my head slightly, which had been lying on Damien's chest, to get a better look at him. It had been about thirty minutes since we properly celebrated our engagement and we had somehow made it to the bedroom we were staying in. "What's that?"

"We're moving back into the mansion. In fact, we should be all moved back in by the time we step foot back in NYC."

I sat up and looked at him in disbelief. There would be no more hiding out in the home in the sky unless I wanted to.

"Thank you," I whispered and leaned over to kiss him softly on the lips. I could feel him growing harder under my leg that was thrown across his body. He deepened the kiss and flipped me on my back.

"Ready for another round?" Damien asked.

"Always."

20

ANAIS

"So, this is where Damien lives when he's not at the penthouse. And now it's your home."

"Wow, I forgot you haven't seen this place yet." Being back in the place I renamed as the NoHo Mansion felt wonderful. We had more space, and I couldn't wait to add pops of color to the place to make it fit a blend of styles versus strictly Damien's. I was drawing from some of the colors and vibrancy that we saw while we were in St. Barts, determined to bring some of paradise home. We had been back in the city for several days and I was already ready to return to the island.

As I showed Ellie around the home, I made a mental note of things I wanted to change or update. I also couldn't stop myself from thinking about changing at least one into a nursery, but that would be a while yet. I wanted Damien to myself for a little while longer before the pattering of baby feet in this home.

One thing I wasn't expecting to be weird that was, was now having access to the main bedroom on the top floor. The room that had been a source of contention early in our relationship was now accessible to me whenever I wanted. It was another room on my list that needed pops of color. I also hoped subtle changes would remove memories of the nightmares that Damien experienced alone. Thankfully, neither one of us were having many nightmares these days.

"Speaking of him, where is Damien?"

"He went into the office when we met up for lunch to get a few things done that he hadn't had time to work on this week."

Ellie nodded, shifting the box she was holding and looked around my newly claimed living room. She had come over to check out my new engagement ring and to help me start making small changes to the NoHo Mansion. "Pretty sure I could fit the apartment in the living room alone."

That triggered a light bulb moment. "We should talk about that. With me moving in with Damien, what are you going to do? How can I help?"

Ellie smiled and said, "Damien offered to let me rent the apartment I've been staying in for a discounted rate. Said I could do it as long as I was friends with you, so now you'll never get rid of me."

I couldn't stop the giggles that left my mouth. "Never imagined I would be able to anyway."

A knock on the door stopped us both from talking. I glanced at Ellie before I walked closer to the front. Damien installed an all-new security system including cameras and other accessories while we were in St. Barts, in order to ensure that he was doing everything to protect me.

"Kingston."

I double-checked that it was indeed him although I recognized his voice before opening the door. We gave each other small smiles before I brought him into the living room where Ellie laid eyes on him.

Her mouth fell open for a split second before she said, "I remember you! You were giving me hell when Anais and I went to Elevate."

Kingston shrugged before crossing his arms. "I have no recollection of that."

"You are so full of—"

"Hey now. You guys need to cut it out because chances are you'll be seeing a lot more of each other." I couldn't say that I didn't find this amusing. Ellie almost looked as if she was going to take off her shoe and aim it at his head while Kingston viewed her coolly, yet a small smile played on his lips. *This is interesting.*

"Damien's going to be home a little late and he couldn't reach you."

Really? It's the weekend and he isn't supposed to be in the office anyway. I pulled out my phone from my back pocket and sure enough, found a text message from Damien stating the same thing.

Damien: *Going to be home later than planned tonight.*

Me: *Sorry I missed this message. Kingston came in and mentioned it. See you when you get home.*

When I put my phone back in my pocket, I looked up to find Ellie glaring at Kingston.

"Have you always been a prick? Or was this behavior saved just for me."

Kingston shrugged. "Just for you."

I could see that Ellie was about to snap back and I

jumped in before she could. "Okay, enough, you two. Kingston, I'll let you know if I need anything else."

Kingston nodded his head and turned to leave but was stopped by Ellie's voice.

"Do you really need a coin to get into the sex club?"

Kingston looked over his shoulder, right at Ellie. "No." And with that, he walked out as quickly as he entered.

"That man is infuriating."

I nodded my head. "And to make matters worse, he hasn't seen one episode of *Friends*. Who does that?"

Ellie raised an eyebrow at me but didn't ask questions. I was thankful that she hadn't. Before I knew it, we were settled on the couch watching a romantic comedy. About halfway through the movie, Ellie needed to get a drink from the kitchen so I paused the movie so she wouldn't miss any of it.

"Things almost feel back to normal," I said as I waited for her to come back from the kitchen. "Granted things have changed, but they are also still the same. Like look, we're watching a movie in the early evening."

"Yep, except it's in a mansion that is probably worth more than anything I will ever own in my life."

I rolled my eyes and shook my head, but she continued.

"Things have changed a lot. Who would have thought you'd be engaged to one of the most notorious bachelors in New York City? Especially after I warned you not to get addicted...although I would say I think he's as equally addicted to you if not more."

"You never know what could happen. Get over here so we can finish this movie."

"I'm coming, I'm coming."

While I waited for Ellie to get back, I checked my phone

again but there were no new notifications. I sent a text message to Damien, asking for an update on when he would arrive home.

Me: *Are you coming home soon?*

Damien: *It'll be a little while yet, but hopefully soon.*

Me: *Okay see you then.*

Once Ellie was seated again, I unpaused the movie and we finished watching it. A glance outside confirmed that it was evening as Ellie stood up to stretch. "I should probably call Nick so that we can head back to my apartment."

As Ellie did that, I checked my phone again but there was nothing from Damien.

"Nick should be outside so I'm going to go."

I put my phone back in my pocket and walked Ellie to the door. I gave her a big hug before opening the door.

"Tell Damien I said hi and that he really did a good job with this engagement ring."

I smiled. "He did, didn't he? I'll let him know."

Kingston came to the front door and Ellie served him with a glare before walking down to the car that Nick was waiting in. With a small wave, I watched as Ellie drove away.

I turned to Kingston and said, "Can we go to Cross Tower? Maybe me showing up there will be enough to get him to leave his stuff at work."

"Sure."

"Also don't tell him. It can be a surprise."

I could see Kingston weighing the choices and he said, "I don't see why not."

"Perfect. I'm ready when you and Rob are."

21

DAMIEN

"Mr. Cross."

"Yes?" I said as I looked up at Melissa, who was standing in the doorway.

"Do you need anything before I head out?"

"No. I've got everything else. Thanks for coming in on your day off. Have a good night."

Melissa lingered for a second before she left, closing the door behind her. I continued reading the briefings that I received while I was out on vacation, trying to get ahead on discussions that were occurring on Monday.

A quick glance at my computer screen told me that an hour had passed since Melissa had left and I was still sitting here answering emails and reading reports. I checked my phone and noticed that I missed a message from Anais when a knock on my office door left me puzzled. *Who is here this late on a Saturday?*

"Who is it?"

"Cleaning."

"Come in."

Just as I said the words, I reminded myself that it was the weekend and that there usually wasn't any member of the cleaning crew here now.

Someone wearing dark clothes, a baseball cap, and dragging a large garbage can opened the door. With my foot, I slowly opened my bottom drawer, not wanting to take any chances having entered an unknown situation.

"It's about time that we met each other in person, Mr. Cross."

I stood up from my chair. "I see you finally got my message, Vincent."

The man in front of me chuckled but it was clear he didn't find what I said funny. He moved farther into the room. "I'm here to collect what is owed to me."

"What? My death?"

"Precisely. I wanted to make you hurt as much as your father made me hurt, but there's been a change in plans."

"Due to the botched kidnapping?"

Vincent shrugged. "Sometimes it's easier to do things yourself. I'll make sure that the job is done right this time. Why don't you take a seat?"

"I'd rather stand."

Vincent pulled a revolver out of his pocket. I raised my hands and he gestured with the gun for me to take a seat. I hesitated before sitting in the chair and I stole a glance at my gun that I started carrying with me after Anais's kidnapping.

"You're going to pay for what happened to my father. Martin Cross is going to understand the pain of losing his own flesh and blood."

"What? Because my father didn't want to bail yours out again?"

"He could have saved his life."

"Not based on what we now know. Your father owed a lot of people money and it was only a matter of time before they came to collect."

"Liar!" Vincent roared and I saw a vein in his forehead that looked like it might burst at any moment. Until he suddenly calmed down. "You are just trying to rile me up. I'm going to enjoy the little game that I have planned."

Although the look in his eyes told me what I was thinking was a bad idea, I decided to try to reason with him. There was a low chance that I would be able to grab my gun in time to protect myself in case he decided to fire. "I know you've been harboring these feelings for a long time, but I swear, my father wasn't responsible for Harvey's death. I have the records that show how my father tried to help yours and—"

"Hey Damien, I wanted to...what the hell?"

My greatest fear became a reality, when I saw Anais's bright smile as she stood in my office doorway.

"It's nice to officially meet you, Anais. How funny it is that we keep bumping into each other." The sinister voice forced Anais's eyes to bounce between me and him.

"I can't say the feeling is mutual and I wouldn't call stalking bumping into each other."

Vincent smirked and glanced back at me and then back at her. "Well, it's nice that you could join us. I was just about to have a conversation with your fiancé before I killed him. Congrats on making everything official, by the way. Saw the ring on social media a couple of days ago."

"What are you doing here, Anais?"

"I had the same question."

"Fuck you." I glared at Vincent, not caring that he was holding a gun directed at me.

"I wanted to surprise you." Anais stuttered over the last word.

"Well, it's nice that you could join us. As I said, I was just about to have a conversation with your fiancé before I killed him."

I could feel Anais watching me before she moved farther into the room. She stood several feet away from me, creating a triangle between the three of us. "Let her go."

"No. Because that would defeat the purpose of the game I want to play. Russian roulette, and it will be starring the two of you. There are six bullets in this gun, five are blanks and one isn't. Which one of you wants to go first?"

My eyes met Anais and I could see the tears already falling from her eyes. Once again, because of me, she was in a predicament that she shouldn't be in. "I will."

"Damien, no." Her voice trembled and I watched as the tears became a steady stream.

"Fire the gun at me."

"No, because that is what you want. Anais is up first."

Because I didn't doubt that he would shoot her first, I leaned down and reached for my gun in my drawer. Before I could grab it, Vincent noticed and pulled the trigger with no hesitation and I slightly jumped at the loud bang, but that's all there was. That gunshot should have been loud enough to alert someone if they were in the vicinity.

Vincent's expression turned demented when he faced Anais. "Looks like you're up next."

There was a stare down between Anais and Vincent for a moment before she turned to me and mouthed, *I love you.* Terror shook me to my core as I watched her turn around and face the man who could be her murderer. Instinct kicked in, and I knew I couldn't let this happen. I thought about going for my gun again, but there was no way to guarantee I would reach it this time. There was also a chance that he would just shoot Anais anyway.

"Shoot me again."

"Damien, please don't."

"If anyone should die tonight out of the two of us, it should be me."

"No."

Before Vincent could choose who to shoot, I darted over to her pushing her out of the way in case it was a live round. When the gun went off, Anais screamed as we both hit the ground, me pulling her on top of me so I took the brunt of the fall. Our bodies ended up closer to the desk, something I was grateful for. Our moment didn't last long because I didn't trust that he wouldn't try to shoot us both while we were down on the floor, so I jumped back up and pulled Anais with me. I made sure she was behind me as I put my body between hers and Vincent's gun.

"Damien, it looks like you're up next and you know I have no problem killing you."

I stood firm as he pulled the trigger again. Shot number three rang out and once again, it was a blank.

Vincent smiled and fired shot number four without announcing it. I heard Anais gasp behind me, and she placed a hand on my back, the touch was trembling with fear.

"Looks like we're down to two remaining shots. Which one could it be?"

A noise near the door distracted Vincent, who turned to look. It was a split-second decision that I had to make, and pushed Anais behind the desk. I grabbed the gun and jumped up, quickly weighing my options before I pulled the trigger. Anais screamed again and Vincent's body hit the floor with a loud thud.

With Vincent's body out of the way, I could see Kingston in the doorway with his gun drawn. Relief filled my body as I realized it was only him and that he had probably done something to cause the distraction.

I looked at Anais and whispered to her, "Are you okay?" I could tell she wasn't as tears fell from her eyes.

She nodded her head, and I took a moment to scan her body with my eyes and hands, making sure that she actually was okay. Then, I pulled her into my arms, enjoying the feel of her body intertwined with mine.

"Everything is fine now, I promise."

After we embraced for several more minutes, my attention was dragged to Kingston who was staring at Vincent's dead body. "What the fuck took you so long?"

"We were downstairs in the car so things were a little muffled. I got suspicious when I hadn't heard anything from Anais. Looks like Uncle Martin needs to overhaul security here because there is no way Vincent should have been able to get up here."

"I'll be sure to let him know."

Kingston walked over to his body and kicked the gun out of the way. He bent down to check to see if there was a pulse.

He looked up at me and said, "He's dead. Looks like both of our shots hit him."

The words I had been waiting to hear since I found out about Vincent were one of the top three things I had ever heard. It was finally over.

"We need to call Will and fill him in. We have a special delivery to make."

22

DAMIEN

I pulled the SUV into a parking garage, in a spot that wasn't well lit by lights. There were no other cars around, but we were expecting at least one to pick up the package we had.

"I'm glad to have this off of our hands." I reached into my pocket and pulled my phone out.

Me: *We're downstairs.*

I looked at Kingston and said, "Drop off should be any minute."

He laid his head on the headrest of the passenger seat. "I'm glad."

"Tired? I thought you worked all of the time?"

"After this shit? A vacation is calling my name."

I snorted. "I would think that is well deserved."

"Yeah, I should take a break before either you or your brothers get into some more shit and call me."

There was a knock on the window closest to me and I turned to look out of it. There I found the man of the hour.

"About time you joined us."

"You better have some good news."

Will's ability to skip the bullshit was one of his greater qualities. "And if I told you I did?"

Will stood up and looked at me. "He's dead?"

I nodded. "I brought him just like I said I would. He's in the trunk."

Will took a step back and Kingston and I got out of the vehicle. A slight breeze filtered through the garage as we walked to the back of the SUV and I popped the trunk. Will waited as Kingston unzipped the body bag and took a look inside it. With a slight nod of his head, Kingston closed the body bag back up and Will stared off into the distance. Kingston walked back toward the passenger side of the car, giving Will and I an opportunity to talk alone.

He was silent for a moment before he said, "You know, I never thought I would be relieved that my brother was dead. Part of me wishes I would have been the one to put the bullet in him."

I thought about my relationship with my own brothers and his statement hit me hard. Having one of my brothers do what Vincent did would be an enormous betrayal, one that I wasn't sure if I would ever get over.

"At least Charlotte doesn't have to live in fear anymore."

Will looked back at me for a second before turning to look off into the distance. "Charlotte will always have to look over her shoulder due to her connection to me, much like Anais will have to because of you. We can do our best to protect the ones we love but that threat is always there, hiding just under the surface. And I'll never forgive myself for failing her."

"How'd you fail her?"

"If I had been here after our father died, she wouldn't have gotten caught up in Vincent's shit. I would have made sure of it. But I was off dealing with my own stuff and I thought everything would be fine here. I was wrong and I'll live with that for the rest of my life."

"You couldn't have known."

Will shook his head and I could see that my words didn't have their intended effect on him. He still blamed himself for what happened.

"Speaking of Charlotte, she's gone."

I narrowed my eyes at Will. "What do you mean she's gone?"

"She left the city again. Of course, this time I know where she went, but out of the abundance of caution and her privacy, I'm keeping it quiet. Being kidnapped and dragged back to New York in addition to everything else that happened...it would be a lot for anyone but even more so for someone who has had to look over her shoulder every time she went somewhere or did anything for over a decade. So, I let my baby sister go again. If it gives her happiness and peace, that's what I want her to have." He slowly turned and faced me again.

I held out my hand. "Everything is settled between us now?"

Will stared at my hand before shaking it. "It is."

"I'm sure we'll be in touch."

"I'm sure we will."

23

ANAIS
ONE MONTH LATER

This red dress looked fantastic on me, but it would be better served on the floor, I thought as I examined the dress from all angles in the mirror. The lacy bodice was mostly see-through, only hiding my nipples before it flared into an A-line skirt that was also sheer. I put on the short red skirt that came with the ensemble under the sheer garment to keep some of my body covered. It was a bit dramatic for an evening at Elevate, but I was in a celebratory mood and this dress called out to me when I picked it up a couple of hours ago. I wore my hair down and added a red lipstick, knowing that it was only a matter of time before this whole look would be ruined anyway.

I grabbed a long black coat and threw it over my arm. It would help give the illusion that I was more covered than I was and only Damien and I knew what I was really wearing underneath.

It was still revealing, yet I felt more empowered than I had in a very long time. I felt as if I was the queen of this kingdom and I had so much power at my fingertips. I regularly brought one of the most powerful men in New York City to his knees and he enjoyed it. I gave myself one final look over and walked toward the elevator. I had no intention of walking down the stairs in these sky-high heels even if the mansion was nowhere near as tall as the penthouse.

Things had quieted down since Damien killed Vincent. We cut the amount of security that my parents, Ellie, and I needed, and life had gone back to some semblance of normal. I decided to go to therapy after the events that took place to have someone to talk to and work through the trauma that I'd dealt with over the last few months. It was one of the best decisions I could make for myself and I was happy I did it.

Damien did end up closing the deal on my office building and I was soon back walking the halls of Monroe Media Agency. It felt good to be working among my coworkers again and to have that social interaction while we were doing our best for our clients. Once word got out about the threat to Damien and me and the aftermath of Vincent's death, business was booming for us. At least something good came out of this treacherous shit show.

When the elevator reached the main level, I walked toward his office where I knew he would be this evening. When I reached the doorway, he didn't look up, even though I assumed he sensed my presence and heard my heels on the floor.

"Ahem."

Damien looked up from the document and saw me standing in the doorway, my outfit on full display. He raised an eyebrow, daring me to continue.

"Take me to Elevate."

"Since when do I take orders for you?" He leaned back in his office chair, lazily taking all of me in. "When did you get this outfit?"

"Sometime within the last month or so but that's none of your concern. I want to go back."

He stood up. "But it is my business seeing as how I—"

"Control my pleasure, I know. An adventure at Elevate would be pleasurable for both of us."

"You know if we go there, we're going to turn it up a bit."

I nodded. "I'm looking forward to it." I turned around to give him an eyeful of the dress. His eyes swallowed me whole and I was willing to bet that he wanted to take me up against the wall right here. In order to prevent that from happening, I turned on my heel and walked down the hallway.

When he followed me into the living room, I noticed he'd unbuttoned the top button of his white shirt. "Are you sure you want to go to Elevate? We could have plenty of fun right here."

"I'm positive. This dress deserves to be stared at."

"As long as all they're looking at is the dress and not the body wearing it. That belongs to me and to me alone."

"That just so happens to be fine by me, Mr. Cross."

"I'm glad we could agree on this subject, Ms. Monroe. No compromising necessary."

"Do you trust me?" Damien asked as I was sitting down on the bed in the room, my dress flowing around me. When we arrived downstairs, Damien picked up a box and led me into this room.

"Of course, what kind of question is that?"

He smiled for a brief moment at my answer before placing the box on the bed next to me and opening it. When he turned around to show me, I gasped.

"You want to blindfold me?"

"Is that a problem?"

"No, Damien." The confidence in my voice thrilled me.

"I also might have a couple other items that will make this more pleasurable. If anything becomes a problem for you, tell me immediately." When I nodded my head he said, "Then let's get started, shall we?"

Damien opted for a non-themed room this time around and it looked like any other bedroom except for the giant mirror on the ceiling. I wondered if he had any plans for it.

"Strip."

That one word made me quiver with desire as I stood up and stared him down while I removed my garments. When I was stark naked in front of him, he gestured for me to sit down on the bed.

"Lie down on your back, legs spread out in front of you."

When I did as he asked, Damien handed me the blindfold and I put it on myself. With the blindfold, this was turning into a completely different experience. With the loss of my eyesight, my other senses strengthened, and I could feel my wetness growing in anticipation for what he had planned.

There was silence in the room, and I waited with bated breath to see if I could hear anything that would clue me into what Damien was doing. Silence was the only thing that greeted me.

"Damien?" I whispered after the silence became too much for me to handle.

"I'm here, Spitfire."

He was here all right. He said the words right in my ear and I felt a shift on the bed due to his added weight.

"I want you to keep your arms above your head until I tell you that you can move them."

I smirked and asked, "And if I don't?" Sassiness dripped from my words and it wasn't too long before he gave an appropriate response.

A nice, firm swat on the ass. I sighed, missing the feeling of that type of contact on my skin. I was tempted to disobey him again to see what he would do, but there was time for that later. "Okay, I won't move."

"Good girl."

His weight shifted once more, and I briefly felt skin-to-skin contact. Had he taken off his clothes too?

I gasped when something light touched my skin. The item brushed along my chest, making sure to pay special attention to my nipples.

"Is that a feather?"

"It is."

I'd never would have thought that the light touch of a feather would have me withering but here I was, trying to guess where he might touch me again. The feather took one final dusting over my nipples before disappearing.

"Good job on not moving your hands." I felt his hands move down my body with the softest of touches, almost reminiscent of the feather that was on my skin just seconds ago. His fingers stopped at my pussy where he lazily dragged a finger up and down my seam. "It looks as if you enjoyed that very much. Let's see if you can do as good of a job with this."

It was a few moments before I felt something cool waiting at my entrance. "What's that?"

Instead of answering, Damien turned it on, and I moaned so loud that it sounded foreign to my own ears. It was a vibrator, but the sensations made any thoughts in my mind vanish. This vibrator was bigger than the one I had used before and it was definitely an example of when bigger is better.

When I felt him tweak one of my nipples, my hips nearly bucked off the bed. I heard a faint dark chuckle over the noise of the vibrator as I felt the beginning of the end start. My body shuddered as an orgasm took over, making me lose all control. My groans and gasps didn't stop Damien's assault on me. He kept the vibrator turned on as I rode out my orgasm.

Suddenly the vibrations stopped, and Damien rubbed my sensitive clit. How I kept my hands in place, I'd never know.

"You don't know how beautiful you just looked as I watched you come hard. But now it's time for you to see it for yourself."

The blindfold was taken off my eyes and it took me a moment to adjust to the light. My eyes found Damien's and saw the look of love gleaming from them. He bent down to kiss me before he positioned himself at my pussy and guided his cock inside of me. He groaned as he pumped into me.

"Look up. I want you to watch yourself as I make you come. You may move your arms."

My eyes slowly moved from him up to the ceiling where I got a front row seat to watching our own personal show live. I watched as he pumped his dick in and out of me, creating an even more intimate connection as our bodies found a rhythm that was just for us. Being able to watch ourselves perform such a sensual and primal act was the most erotic thing I had ever seen. And then Damien's eyes met mine in the mirror. Watching the look on his face as his thrust met one of mine painted a beautiful scene of our love.

I could feel another orgasm building within me just as Damien sped up the pace, telling me that he was getting closer to the edge as well. I bit my lip when I saw him briefly close his eyes as he continued fucking me.

"I'm going to come," he announced as he looked down at me, but my eyes were fixated on the mirror above.

I shouted first as my release charged through me and not once did Damien stop his motions until he joined me on the other side of his orgasm.

Sweat and heavy breathing were shared between us before I said, "That was extraordinary. I'm just in awe."

"And to think that this is just the beginning, Spitfire." He wiped away one lonely happy tear that fell from my eye.

"I love you."

"And I love you too."

"Think your mother is having enough fun with this?"

"Oh, this?" Damien snorted. "She's just getting started. This is why I said we should just tell her how we envisioned it and she will take it from there."

"You were right...again."

"I'm still not used to hearing that."

I flipped my hair over my shoulder. "Good. Don't."

Damien reached down and patted my butt. Even though the pat was light, and my gown stood between him touching me, I was thinking about the moments we spent the night before and how I couldn't wait to get out of here to do it all over again.

"Stop looking like that."

I turned to Damien. "Looking like what?"

"Like you want me to bend you over right now and welcome our guests with a real show."

I chuckled. "That would be quite the show."

"Oscar worthy, although it wouldn't be acting."

"Damien, there you are." Selena Cross floated into the room wearing a beautiful gray dress. Not a hair was out of place and she looked at ease even with all of the craziness that was currently going on. Since she was running the show with a team of planners, that might have helped. "Martin is looking for you. He's in the office."

He turned to me and placed a kiss on my lips. His mother patted him on the shoulder just before he gave what could be described as a small smile before he walked away.

"I wanted to come over and say congratulations and welcome to the family." She opened her arms and I stepped into her embrace.

"Thank you, although not quite yet. We need to take our vows."

"I consider you part of the family." She pulled away and looked at my gown. "This is absolutely stunning." The strapless eggplant-colored dress that I was wearing tonight was fitted to my body like a second skin. I accessorized with other purple items and decided to wear my hair up in a low bun for the night.

"And I love yours."

"Thank you, I picked it out just for this evening. I thought it would be on the safer end and wouldn't clash in any of the family photos."

That's right. There probably would be a lot of photos taken and a lot of people here. The thought made my stomach twist a couple of times, but I tamped it down by thinking about how all of this would be over soon.

The Cross estate had been completely transformed into a spring oasis that was stunning. Soft cream-colored flowers, many of them roses and tulips, were all over the home and the layout of the home was converted to fit what had to be at least one hundred people here tonight. I wasn't looking forward to it.

"Damien mentioned that you weren't too crazy about all of the attention."

I shrugged. "It's not my forte, but I know some of it comes with the territory of being with Damien, so I'll deal. Plus, it might mean more business for Monroe Media Agency, which would be a great thing."

"Another reason why you and my son are a great match." Her words confused me, and I must have been wearing it on my face because she chuckled before she said, "You both think strategically and balance each other well. I knew that when you came and stayed with us for a few days, and I watched how you two interacted. I hoped things would lead down to this path with you two getting married, but I didn't want to push. Now here we are."

"Now here we are," I whispered and gave her a small smile. "Thank you."

"You're welcome."

"Okay, Mom. I want some more time with my fiancée."

"All right, even though you've had plenty of time with her. Given the fact that you guys have just come back from vacation again."

That was true. Damien had taken me to Paris after I mentioned wanting to go. It was somewhat of a working vacation because we both held business meetings while there. But once work was done, we spent the rest of the time enjoying one another.

When Bernard opened the front door, Broderick and Gage walked in. It was fascinating to look at all four Cross men in their suits prepared for the night's events.

"If you all aren't a dapper bunch?"

"Dapper? Really, Mom?"

I snickered at Gage's response.

Selena patted him on the arm and said, "We should get ready because our guests will start arriving in a few minutes."

Damien grabbed my hand and gave me a gentle squeeze before he rubbed my knuckles. I smiled up at him, happy to have his company to get through this night. True to Selena's word, people started arriving a few minutes after we separated.

My parents were one of the first to arrive and when they reached me, they gave me a big hug. Dad was doing much better and was almost back to being one hundred percent. Mom was doing well too, and Dad was planning on taking her on vacation in a couple of weeks to give not just both of them an opportunity to relax, but to thank her for everything that she did when he was recovering from getting shot.

"You look beautiful, sweetheart." Mom held both hands on my arms and she took a piece of my hair that had gone astray and placed it behind my ear. It was a habit she developed when I was a toddler, and she did it on occasion even though I was an adult. As a teenager, it annoyed me, but now I realized she was only trying to help.

"Your mother is right. You look stunning." He leaned over and placed a kiss on my cheek. He then turned to Damien and shook his hand. "It's nice to see you."

I appreciated Dad being polite although I don't know if he

had completely warmed up to Damien as of yet. I felt bad for telling him that little white lie about whether or not Damien and I were involved, but I was happy to see that he seemed to be moving past it.

The four of us quietly talked until I heard my name from across the room. I turned and found Ellie walking up to me. When she reached me, she gave me a tight hug before grabbing my left hand. "I still can't believe you're engaged!" She dropped my hand and pulled me into her arms for a quick hug.

I chuckled. "You say that every time we see each other in person."

"I know but I still can't believe it. Is this the part where I threaten Damien?"

"I would suggest not doing that, Ms. Winters."

I wondered if I was the only one who knew he was joking based on the looks on my parents' and Ellie's faces. "He's kidding."

The sigh of relief that everyone released made me nudge Damien. He looked at me but said nothing.

"Hi Anais and Damien."

Our attention was diverted once more when Grace walked up to us, greeting us. I quickly introduced her to Ellie and my parents. After that was done, the group started to have a round of small talk. I looked around to see if someone in particular had spotted who had just arrived. *Bingo.* Broderick's attention was completely on Grace, even as his twin was talking to him. It was a few seconds before Broderick noticed me looking at him but it didn't matter anyway because he just shrugged and turned his attention back to Gage.

"Interesting," I muttered.

"What's interesting?" Damien whispered in my ear.

"Nothing, nothing important." I turned to face him, pulling him closer to me by his lapels. "Let's enjoy this night that was put together in honor of us."

"Oh. So, are you finally saying you're mine?"

"No." I paused. "I'm finally saying that *you* are mine."

Damien shook his head and gave me a kiss on my lips. It held promises of what was to come later tonight once we were alone. He grabbed my hand and pulled me through the crowd until we reached a makeshift stage. First, he helped me up and then he followed suit. Broderick, who was standing on this side of the room, handed Damien a microphone but Martin Cross got up on the stage with another microphone in hand.

"Excuse me." Martin waited a beat before he continued. "First I want to thank everyone for coming to celebrate my son Damien and his fiancée, Anais."

A round of applause could be heard in all corners of the room, making me want to slink away, but I refused. I belonged here. This party was to celebrate my upcoming nuptials with Damien. And dammit, I was doing just that.

"I also want to thank my wife, Selena, and Anais's mother, Ilaria, and the wonderful staff here to help pull all this together." The room clapped once more. "Now, I want to introduce my oldest son, Damien."

I tried to control the rush of emotions that I could feel creeping up my face as Damien held out his hand for me and together, we walked toward the center of the stage. "Thanks, Dad." He smiled at his dad before squeezing my hand.

I took several deep breaths as the crowd quieted down and Damien turned to me.

"First I want to thank everyone for coming out this evening. It means a lot that you're here to celebrate us. I never knew what it meant to love someone. I did my best to avoid anything related to a significant other or finding a partner for life. Until I met Anais, I thought I had everything even though there was always a nagging feeling in the back of my mind. She was what I was missing." He smiled at me. "It was always you. Thank you for changing my life for the better and I can't wait to make you my wife. And if anyone knows me well enough, you know how impatient I am so don't be shocked if we get married tomorrow morning."

A light chuckle rippled through the crowd. It was clear that Damien was telling a joke...right?

SOMETIME LATER, I was washing my hands in the bathroom after fixing up my makeup. Taking so many photos and talking to so many people had taken its toll on the state of my face, so a quick touch-up was required. As I was getting ready to walk out the door and rejoin the party, a voice made me stop.

"Stop being an asshole. I don't have to explain myself to you."

"When you are standing there flirting with that fucker, the hell you do."

"What business is it of yours who I flirt with? What has gotten into you?"

"It became my business when you—Grace. Grace!"

I thought it was Broderick who screamed her name. *What is that about?*

I waited a few more seconds before I walked out of my hiding place once I thought the coast might be clear.

"There you are."

I turned and found my husband-to-be with a soft smile playing on his lips.

"My trip to the bathroom took a little longer than usual."

"Did it have anything to do with Broderick and Grace? I saw them standing nearby when I walked out to find you."

"Maybe." I sang the word in a whimsical voice that made Damien chuckle.

"Whatever is going on between them is none of your concern."

"Speak for yourself. Now that I'm not getting kidnapped or shot at, I have plenty of time to worry about what is going on with the people around me."

He leaned over to give me a kiss before he whispered in my ear, "And I can't wait to punish you for that smart mouth later."

The End

THANK you for reading Steel Empire! While Anais and Damien's trilogy is complete, the Broken Cross series continues with Shadow Empire, Broderick and Grace's book. Keep reading to find a sneak peek of it!

. . .

DON'T WANT to let Anais and Damien go just yet. Click HERE to grab a bonus scene featuring the couple!

WANT to join discussions about the Broken Cross Series? Click HERE to join my Reader Group on Facebook.

PLEASE JOIN my newsletter to find out the latest about the Broken Cross series and my other books!

SHADOW EMPIRE BLURB

What lurks in the shadows...

I was in the wrong place at the wrong time
When Broderick Cross saved me from an untimely fate.
I hated him with every fiber of my being,
And I know he won't touch me because I'm his best friend's sister.
Or that's what I thought.
But even with danger knocking on my door,
The one I need protection from is him.

SNEAK PEEK OF SHADOW EMPIRE
GRACE

I hated that son of a bitch with every inch of my being.

Our eyes met as soon as I entered the bar. Not even the darkness of the environment could prevent the stare down that occurred. Blue eyes clashed with brown and warning bells sounded in my mind.

It was the first time I had seen Broderick in person since we last spoke at Damien and Anais's engagement celebration. I was shocked to be invited but was glad to attend and celebrate the happy couple and seeing some familiar faces was usually great, especially when you're attending an event alone. Here I was hoping to enjoy a night off when I didn't have anything going on, but of course, Broderick Cross showed up to this party as well.

Broderick had been in my life for as long as I could remember. At times I was just seen as just the younger sister who followed them around when we were younger. That faded as we got older and I would see Broderick more on occasion while I was in high school and in college.

Normally, our relationship was on good terms. It wasn't

unheard of that I would watch football with him and my brother when I was free. That was all ruined the night he tried to take control over who I could and couldn't speak to. I rolled my eyes and turned away, choosing to fall deeper into the crowded bar, hoping to blend in and find my brother at the same time.

I shouldn't have been surprised. My brother was hosting a party, so the chances of Broderick attending were high. The only way it would have been higher was if Hunter had asked to host the party at Elevate. After all, the two of them had been thick as thieves for decades. Deep down I knew there was a good chance that he would show up, but I also didn't want to miss out on an evening of fun all because Broderick had decided to be a prick several weeks ago.

My work schedule sometimes meant long hours and while my job was mostly rewarding, it had its drawbacks too. Tonight, I had an opportunity to relax and here he was attempting to insert himself into my night after I told him to get lost the last time that I saw him.

While I was at Damien and Anais's engagement party, I struck up a conversation with a man in attendance. The conversation was friendly at best and Broderick came over fuming. The whole incident was very dramatic, and I was over it. I didn't need Broderick trying to protect me as if he were my older brother. Not now, not ever.

I pulled at the dark denim jacket that I had thrown on over my low-cut black shirt and jeans with black flats. The perfect outfit for me for this spring evening. I tucked a piece of my blonde hair behind my ear and smiled at the bartender when I approached. I ordered a light beer and received it immediately, basking in the fact that I didn't have to pay due to my brother having an open bar.

"There's my favorite little sister."

I smiled at the moniker. "I'm your only little sister," I said as I turned around. There standing behind me was my older brother, IPA in hand, ready to be the life of the party.

"I'm glad you could make it."

"Same, but I wouldn't miss your promotion celebration for the world. I'm so proud of you."

I leaned in to hug him and when I looked over his shoulder, I saw the only person who was currently on my shit list.

"Hey, man, congrats on the promotion."

Broderick came around Hunter's left side while I stood on his right. It took everything in me not to roll my eyes. I waved my brother off when one of his friends called his name and all that was left were two piercing blue eyes staring back at me.

"Grace."

I let out a deep breath. "I don't want to talk to you."

"Tough shit. I want to talk to you."

He has some damn nerve. I leaned over and whispered to him, "I'm not talking to you about anything related to my personal life because it is none of your concern. Better yet, I don't want to talk to you at all. So leave."

That didn't do anything to deter him. "Hellion, if you want to experience Elevate up close and personal, all you had to do was ask. Not entertain the idea of some asshole in a cheap three-piece suit taking you there."

My mood soured. Broderick had the audacity to say these things, but I refused to sit here and tolerate it. I took another swig of my beer before I put the beer back down on the bar before I turned to him. "Who knew how much of an asshole you could be? Wait, don't answer that. Have a good night."

I hoped the bite in my tone told him that I wanted him to have anything but. I made my way through the crowd and found my brother.

"Listen, Hunt, something came up and I need to head out," I whispered in his ear.

"Already?" The look of disappointment made me feel like shit, but I knew if I stayed, Broderick would be watching me like a hawk all night. I also didn't trust myself not to snap at him again. Hunter opened his arms and I stepped inside of his embrace. "Do you want me to walk you to the subway?"

I shook my head. "No. Don't miss out on your own party because of me. I might decide to take a cab. I'll call you later."

"You better."

I gave him one final smile before I strolled toward the door. Just before I reached it, I looked up and found Broderick staring back at me from another corner of the room. He lifted his beer in a mock salute, and I gave him my one-finger one in return. Two can play this immaturity game.

I pulled out my phone to call a car and saw that the wait time was way longer than I wanted to deal with. I adjusted my jacket over my body, applied a coat of lip gloss on my lips, and put my phone back in my purse before I wandered down the street. I walked a couple of buildings away from the bar before I heard a low groan coming from my left. When I looked, I found a dimly lit alleyway, but I saw nothing from darkness.

Is someone over there? Where had that noise come from?

Although fear swam through my mind, I knew I had to do something. That was when I saw someone leaning against a brick wall and it was clear that they were hurting in some way. As I started to walk into the alley, another figure appeared from the shadows and walked up to the person and the next thing I heard was a croak. The figure backed away from the person, who slowly slid down the brick wall.

Did...did I just see someone get stabbed?

A scream bubbled below the surface and I knew if it erupted from my mouth, I would draw the attention of the person still in the alleyway. Before I could open my mouth or run away, something covered my mouth and dragged me away from the alley. That something felt warm against my lips. Since I still had the ability to fight, there was no way I was going down without one. I fought against my attacker and I heard a grunt before someone said, "Grace, cut it out."

Broderick?

"Let me go!" I screamed, but it was mostly muffled by what I now knew to be Broderick's hand.

He continued pulling me back until he whispered in my ear, "I'm going to remove my hand, but you have to promise not to scream."

I nodded my head quickly and he did as he said he would. As he wiped his hand, removing the remnants of my lip gloss from it, I said, "Broderick, I might be able to save his life, let me go."

"Do you want to save your own? Be quiet and follow me."

Shadow Empire is available for pre-order and will be released in Summer 2021.

ABOUT THE AUTHOR

Bri loves a good romance, especially ones that involve a hot anti-hero. That is why she likes to turn the dial up a notch with her own writing. Her Broken Cross series is her debut dark romance series.

She spends most of her time hanging out with her family, plotting her next novel, or reading books by other romance authors.

https://www.facebook.com/briblackwoodwrites

ALSO BY BRI BLACKWOOD

Broken Cross Series

Sinners Empire (Prequel)

Savage Empire

Scarred Empire

Steel Empire

Shadow Empire

Made in the USA
Las Vegas, NV
30 August 2022

54391763R00132